FRACTURED

THE ARC SERIES BOOK THREE

ALEXANDRA MOODY

Edited by Pete Thompson
Cover Design by Alexandra Moody

ISBN-13: 978-1519200426
ISBN-10: 1519200420

For Pete.

CHAPTER ONE

I wake to a high-pitched, repetitious beeping noise and the strong stench of disinfectant. The bitter odour tingles my nose, tempting me to sneeze. In my sleepy haze I lift my hand to rub at the prickling sensation. But as I do, I feel something hard attached to the back of my hand.

My eyes fly open as I jerk my hand away from my face. At first, my vision is blurry and the bright world around me is an array of indistinct blobs. It gradually clears, but this does nothing to settle my confusion. A long tube extends from my hand to a machine beside the bed, which dispenses a clear liquid into it.

Where the hell am I?

There's a dull ache in the back of my head. My mouth is dry and there's a strange metallic taste on the tip of my tongue. I don't feel like myself at all. My regular clothes are gone. Instead, I'm dressed in a thin blue gown that reaches down to my knees.

I struggle to push my heavy body up in bed to look around. Clean, white tiles and stark, white walls frame the cold and bare room I'm in. There are no windows and harsh white lights shine down from above making it unnaturally bright in here.

This place feels all too familiar and though I've never been in this room before, it has the same sterile look and suffocating feel to it as the last place I want to be. I must be back in the ARC.

The enclosed white space rattles me more than I would like and my breathing becomes shallow as I try to process my return underground. I had risked so much to escape this place and go after Sebastian. I gave up everything to journey to the mysterious Hope City and find him. I try to remain calm, but I'm slowly starting to freak out.

Why would they bring me back here? Did they figure out I escaped?

I close my eyes and take a deep breath as I try to recall what happened before I went to sleep. My thoughts are muddled though, and the details of my memories flutter just out of my grasp. Why can't I remember?

The last thing I clearly remember was being at school. Recruiters had just arrived and I was trying to get out of there with Hunter. I don't know what happened after we left though and everything is hazy.

Did the recruiters find me? Did they discover I don't belong on the surface and return me underground? Trying to dredge up memories that would rather stay hidden makes my pulse run quicker. It shouldn't be this hard to recall my last waking hours.

I open my eyes to check my CommuCuff, hoping to find some information about the last few hours of my life there. The memory has been wiped though and is as empty as my own. I tap the clear glass surface again, attempting to access the cuff history, but it's all gone and even my contacts have disappeared.

Looking to the door at the end of the room, I can see one of those slick metal security pads mounted on the wall next to it. Over the doorway are two small dark glass cylinders, which I suspect house cameras inside. I want to get a closer look, but I can't go anywhere while this tube links me to the machine at my bedside.

My pulse races as I consider the domes. Who is watching me? But, more importantly, why?

A shudder runs down my spine at the thought, but I push the questions out of my mind to focus on my current task. I raise my arm to inspect the tube attached to the back of my hand. It doesn't look particularly difficult to remove. I'm sure if I just give it a strong tug ... I suck a pained breath in through my teeth as I yank the tube out and throw the cursed thing away from me.

Blood slowly drips down my hand from where the tube had entered the skin. I clamp my other hand over the bleed and swing my legs off the bed to stand. The movement causes a sudden rush of blood away from my head making me sway unsteadily on my feet.

I reach out and grasp the bedhead. The edges of my vision are still blurry and the walls in the room aren't as solid as they should be. Holding my arm out, I use the wall for support as I stagger over to the door.

It's freezing out of the bed, with only the thin gown I'm wearing. The ground is cold beneath my bare feet and the draft that comes in under the doorway bites against my skin.

I'd always intended to return to the ARC, if I could, but not like this. Not stolen away, without a choice, without finding Sebastian to bring him home. An angry tear finds its way down my cheek. My short life on the surface had been on borrowed time. I was never talented like the others. I was never meant to be there and I knew that.

I just hoped I would have longer, a chance at least to see the sun, high overhead, one last time. To say goodbye to the friends who had helped me attempt to find Sebastian. Will Hunter and Lara have any idea what happened to me? Would April even care I'm gone?

The last thought slips in unbidden. There was a time when I knew without doubt the answer to that question, but now? Well, April has become a different person up here. I guess we have both changed.

I place one hand around the handle to pull the door open, but it won't move. The door is locked.

'Hello?' I croak, my voice rough from disuse. 'Is anyone there?' I tap my hand against the cold metal door then place my ear up against it. I don't hear any movement beyond it though.

'Hello?' I call out, one more time. Still, no one answers.

I slowly ease my way back to the lone bed and sit down on the edge of it. Again, I am hit by the strangeness of all this. Why am I in here? Why don't I remember anything? My memories only reach as far as yesterday afternoon. *Hell*, I hope it was yesterday afternoon. What has happened since then?

I hear a scraping noise outside the door and several clicks as the bolts unlock. The hinges groan as the door opens and in through the doorway steps a woman. She's wearing a long white lab coat and has a stethoscope hanging around her neck. I crane my neck to see what is on the other side of the door behind her. I catch sight of a man in black standing in a white hallway beyond, but the door is slammed shut before I can get a good look at him.

The woman approaches my bed. 'Good morning Elle,' she says, as she takes my wrist with her icy hands to bump my cuff against the sensor on her tablet.

'How are you feeling?' she asks, her eyes giving me the barest acknowledgement as they flick up to look at me, before returning to stare at the screen.

She drops my wrist and I wrap my arms around my body. 'I ... ah. I feel fine?'

The woman moves to check my temperature.

'Except, how did I get here? Where are we? Why am I here?' Panic rises inside me, as the questions continue to pour out. 'Who are you? Why don't I remember anything?'

'You're in the hospital. I'm the nurse on duty and you're here to get better,' she says.

'But, I'm not sick. There's been some sort of mistake.' I try to stand, but the nurse firmly places one hand on my shoulder.

'There hasn't been a mistake,' she replies. 'I'm afraid you are sick. I will take you to the doctor after I've finished examining you. He'll be able to answer your questions.'

'I'm sick?' I whisper, a wave of doubt rushing through me. The nurse seems certain. 'What's wrong with me?'

'The doctor will explain further,' she says, lifting her hand off my shoulder and pulling the stethoscope from around her neck.

I become increasingly tense as she checks me over. The lady is trying to be gentle with me and is saying all the right things, but her shoulders are rigid and her eyes alert. There's something off about this whole situation and I don't like it one bit.

The nurse pulls back from me and stands straight. 'I will take you to the doctor now. Would you like me to fetch a wheelchair?'

'I can walk,' I reply, standing and decidedly ignoring how dizzy the small movement makes me feel.

'Suit yourself,' she replies.

The woman taps her cuff against the security pad and there's a heavy click as the bolts on the door retract and the door opens. The man in the black suit I'd spotted earlier stands just outside the doorway. He doesn't make eye contact with me, though the nurse gives him a slight shake of her head to which he gives a small nod in return.

He steps back, allowing us to pass. As I follow the woman into the long corridor I glance over my shoulder at the man. He doesn't follow, instead moving off in the other direction.

I want to ask the nurse why he was there, but I stay silent. I suspect she won't answer and that his presence had a whole lot to do with the locked room I found myself in.

'Keep up,' the nurse calls, the sound more distant than I would've expected. I turn and find I've already fallen far behind and stagger to catch up with her.

Like the room I was in, there are no windows anywhere to be seen and only artificial light guides our way as we move through the building. I had hoped there would be windows out here and maybe I was wrong to think I was back in the ARC, but the corridor only proves my first instinct was right.

The place is eerily quiet, with the exception of the incessant tapping of the nurse's shoes against the tiled floor. My own bare feet barely make a sound. The hospital in the ARC was usually abuzz with activity, but this place is more like a morgue than a hospital. It just *feels* wrong.

The nurse knocks on one of the doors and opens it a crack, poking her head inside. 'Dr. Milton, I have Elle Winters here to see you,' she says. 'Are you ready for her?'

'Yes. Send her in,' a man responds.

The door swings wide and I am ushered into an office. A large wooden desk, covered with thick medical texts, dominates the centre of the room and behind sits an older man. He barely registers I've entered and it seems like his mind is somewhere else entirely. His forehead is creased from too many years of frowning, and his eyes squint as he strains to read the book in his hands.

'You can sit down,' he says, abruptly, causing me to scurry to the closest chair. He runs a hand through his greying hair, but doesn't acknowledge me as he continues to focus on his book.

When he doesn't say a word to me after several minutes of waiting, I begin the conversation. 'Can you tell me what's wrong with me?' I ask. My words don't come out as strong as I'd hoped. I sound weary and the nerves I'm trying so hard to keep at bay sneak in, making my voice tremble.

He looks up, a flicker of annoyance crossing his features that suggests I've spoken out of turn. 'Elle, I'm glad to see you're finally awake,' he says.

I look the man up and down. His words are said pleasantly enough, but there's a wariness to his eyes that makes me cautious of him. 'Why have I been brought here?' I ask.

He shifts back into his chair, crossing one leg. 'You had a routine check up and we noticed some irregularities in your blood work.'

'But I've never had a check up...' my voice trails off. My memories are murky. Maybe I did have one? It doesn't seem right though. Getting a check up is the last thing I'd do. I wouldn't risk them finding out the truth about my lack of talent. Why can't I remember?

'Yes, you had one yesterday. You were struggling to sleep last night so they administered a sedative, which can make things a little muddled for a few days. Your memories will come back to you in time.'

'Sedative?' I shake my head. 'But I'm not sick. There must have been a mistake. I'm not supposed to be here.'

He doesn't take a moment to even consider what I've said before responding. 'I can assure you, you are. It will only get worse if you don't get our help.' There's genuine concern on his face, which is difficult to ignore.

'What do you think is wrong with me?' I ask.

'It seems you were taken to the surface too early. With the increased Lysartium exposure, your cells are mutating too fast,' he explains, talking slowly to make sure I understand.

I swallow uncomfortably, not liking what I hear. 'What does that mean?'

The doctor's eyes soften. 'It means if we don't do something you will get sick.'

'How sick?' I ask, my voice becoming quiet. I can practically feel my nerves crackling in the air around me.

'Sick enough that you won't be able to leave your bed. You won't be able to go to school or see your friends. Your headaches will become increasingly worse, you'll lose your appetite and the little food you do get down, you'll throw up. The mental stability of patients with your symptoms has been known to deteriorate...' he pauses, his eyes weighing me up before he continues. 'Without treatment your illness is terminal.'

'What?' My voice sounds frail and my body feels weak. He thinks I'm dying? 'You can make me better, right?'

'That depends on how you respond to our therapies. We'd like to run a few tests, if that's okay with you?'

'Tests?' I hesitate. 'I ... I'm not sure.'

'If we don't do them you're only going to get worse.'

'I don't even feel sick.' Maybe a little tired, but not sick. This can't be happening. This isn't real.

The doctor shakes his head. 'You're only in the early stages. If you get our help now, we can stop the progression. If not ... well, it won't be good.'

I fold my arms across my chest and struggle to take in a deep breath. My body shakes as the air moves down into my lungs and then out again. 'And the treatment will work?'

'Yes.'

My gaze drops to stare at the medical text lying open in front of him. There's a large, colourful picture of a DNA molecule on one page, with lots of writing on the other.

'Elle?' he asks.

I don't know what to say to him. I don't know what to think. All I can seem to do is focus on the bright blue and red strands of the molecule on the page.

'Elle, it's best if we start the treatment as soon as possible.'

I aimlessly nod, as his words pour over me, not really hearing and not really listening either. He keeps on talking, but I have no idea what he's saying. There are no words that can change the prognosis he's given me. I don't want to be sick and I definitely don't want treatment or any tests. I just want to leave this place.

'Are you happy to start the treatment?' he asks, his words finally cutting through the fog that clouds my mind. I recoil back into the chair.

'I'm not sure,' I whisper. This is all happening so quickly.

He doesn't respond immediately and, when I look up at him, he appears annoyed by my response. 'We should start straight away. The sooner we can administer the gene therapy, the better odds you have of making a full recovery'

I nod in response. 'Okay. You can start the treatment.'

'You're making the right choice.' He flips the book shut on his desk, his cool confidence quickly covering the moment of anger I'd caught in his eyes before. He places his lips to his cuff, to let his team of doctors know I'm ready. The way he addresses them, it's as though they had been waiting for me. As though they had already been certain of my answer. When the nurse enters the room to collect me mere seconds later, I wonder if I ever had a choice.

I sigh and take a moment, before I move to follow the woman from the room. 'I never thought I'd be back here,' I say, melancholy as I take in the generic white room around me.

The doctor, who has already turned his back to me, freezes. His shoulders tense and he slowly turns around. 'What are you talking about?' he asks, his face a total mask.

I frown. 'I never thought I'd see the ARC again.'

'The ARC?' he questions. He lets out a small laugh when I nod, his shoulders relaxing. 'Child, you are not in the ARC. You're in West Hope Hospital. No one returns to the ARC.'

CHAPTER TWO

It's evening by the time the doctors finish with me, and I feel more pincushion than human as the nurse leads me back to my room. I can't for the life of me understand why they needed to take so much blood. My skin has turned so pale I'm surprised I have any left.

At least I'm not back in the ARC, although after the news the doctor told me earlier I think I'd rather return underground. I blow out a long, drawn-out breath and try to remain calm. These people know what they're doing and everything will be okay.

My attention wavers as we walk and I struggle to keep myself upright. I feel woozy and quite sleepy now. I almost wish I'd taken the nurse up on the wheelchair offer. *Almost.*

'You will be staying in a ward with other young people,' the nurse explains, as we walk down one of the corridors. It's just as abnormally quiet here as I'd found the walkways earlier today and I am yet to see a window anywhere.

I try to memorise the way we walk, to gain some bearing on where everything is, but this place is a maze. Each corridor is identical to the next, with no numbers or signs over the doors indicating what is in each room. How the nurse can find her way in here is a mystery to me.

'There are others here sick like me?' I ask.

She nods. 'Yes, there are, though not all have the same diagnosis as you.'

'What's wrong with the others?'

The woman looks away from me, to the door we walk towards at the far end of the corridor. 'There's a variety of different things we're treating,' she replies, before falling silent and upping her pace just enough that I struggle to keep up.

She seems reluctant to engage in conversation after my question, but I press on. 'When will I be able to contact my friends and foster family on the outside?'

She chews down on the corner of her lip. 'This is a quarantined area and we don't allow visitors. Dr. Milton would have already spoken with your foster family when you were admitted, so they know you're safe and being taken care of.'

'But I can't talk to them,' I surmise.

She refuses to meet my gaze. 'You'll have to check with Dr. Milton. For now, you should just focus on your treatments.' She slows and approaches one of the doors, tapping her cuff against the security sensor by the doorhandle.

'Just in here, Elle,' she says, pushing the door wide.

Inside is a large room with two rows of metal-framed beds that extend along the walls to the end of the room. Next to each bed is a machine similar to the one I'd been hooked up to earlier this morning, but on closer inspection there is one small difference. Instead of one, there are two cylinders protruding from the metal contraptions. One has the same clear liquid that was pumping into my skin earlier, but my gaze is immediately drawn to the other, which is filled with a bright purple liquid.

I watch the liquid in the machine closest to me as it moves from the cylinder and up the long tube, then into the skin of the child who sits on the bed next to the door. She can't be more than five years old, but she doesn't seem bothered by it in the slightest. Instead, her inquisitive blue eyes are glued to me as I enter the room. All their eyes are.

There are kids and teenagers in here of varying ages. Most of them are in bed, though there are a few younger children playing quietly with the bright array of toys at the far end of the room.

For a place filled with so many children, there's a solemn air to the room I wouldn't have expected. The few that talk to each other do so in hushed whispers and I haven't heard so much as a laugh since the door opened.

I follow the woman down the middle aisle between the beds until we reach an empty one near the back of the room. On one side sleeps a boy who looks to be a couple of years younger than me, but the bed on the other side is empty.

I lower myself to sit on the edge of the bed and face the nurse. It's a struggle for me to not immediately collapse. I'm so much more exhausted than I realised and the promise of sleep the bed offers is too tempting to ignore.

Today has been an emotional rollercoaster and I've barely been able to come to terms with everything the doctor told me. I don't want to even think about it, let alone accept it. Yesterday I was fine and today I'm told I will die if I don't get help from these people.

'We'll do our next round of check ups in the morning,' the nurse says to me. 'If something feels wrong or you need anything, press that big red button on the control panel next to your bed.' She lifts her chin in the direction of a panel secured to the wall to the right of the bed.

'Do you need anything before I leave?' she asks.

I shake my head. 'Just some sleep,' I say, stifling a yawn.

'Okay, we'll see you in the morning,' she replies. She gives me a reassuring smile and then moves away, heading towards the door we entered through earlier. 'Lights out soon,' she calls, as her hand wraps around the handle.

As soon as the door shuts behind her, the room becomes filled with whispers and more than a few sly glances my way. It's as though the place had been on pause whilst the nurse was in here and as soon as she left someone hit play.

I catch one or two phrases of what the others say, but I don't need to hear their words to know what they're talking about. After seeing how they looked at me as I entered the ward, it's clear I'm the source of their whisperings.

I plan to ask the kids in here about the hospital, but before I can leave my bed and approach them, the lights dim and slowly fade to black. The whispers stop and the only sound left in the room are the softly beeping machines.

My tired eyes try to blink back my exhaustion. There are so many questions I still need answering, but I can feel my weariness deep in my bones. As I drift off, my gaze focuses on the machine next to my bed and the vials protruding from the face of it. My last waking thought is of how the strange purple liquid faintly glows in the darkness.

THE BLINDING LIGHTS overhead rudely flicker on early in the morning. I look at my cuff and see it's only 5 A.M. The room erupts in a series of groans as kids throw blankets over their faces and others rub their eyes with their fists. I join the camp of kids who are throwing their blankets over their heads.

I hear the door at the end of the room open, and I peek out from under my blanket, blinking my eyes as they adjust to the light. The nurse from yesterday is back and she sets about checking on the patients in here, starting with the young girl in the bed closest to the door.

'They turn the lights back off after they've checked on everyone,' the boy next to me says, catching me peeking from under the blanket.

I slowly push the covers down and pull myself up in bed. 'It's not exactly an ideal way to wake up,' I grumble. 'Do they do this every morning?'

'Unfortunately,' he replies, though he doesn't look nearly as irritated by the whole early wake up call as I feel. In fact, he looks pretty chipper about the whole ordeal.

I'm curious to ask what's wrong with him and how he ended up in here, but I'm uncertain how to broach the subject. So, instead I ask, 'Have you been here long?'

'Almost a month.'

'A month! Isn't that a long time?'

'Not in here it isn't. Some of the patients have been here for over a year,' he says, dropping his voice low and nodding in the direction of the boy still sleeping in the bed next to him.

The boy is incredibly pale and blue veins stand out visibly on his arms. He looks like he needs to be in a hospital, a lot more than the boy I'm talking to who doesn't seem sick at all.

The nurse approaches my bed and bumps my cuff against her tablet. 'How are you feeling today?' she asks, as she checks the settings on the machine beside my bed.

'Fine.'

She pauses to search my eyes. 'Are you sure?'

'Yeah, totally fine.' Physically, at least. Mentally, I'm still trying to process what's happening to me and I'd rather go back to sleep than try to think about that.

She continues to examine me and when she's finished she moves on to check the boy I've been talking to. He doesn't complain as she pokes and prods at him, even though she does spend a lot longer with him than with me.

Once the nurse moves on he turns to me again. 'I'm Will,' he says, reaching out his hand to me across the gap between our beds.

'Elle,' I reply, giving his hand a brief shake.

'I suspect we're going to be stuck next to each other for a while,' he says. 'May as well get to know one another.'

I flash him a quick smile before sinking back into bed. His words are like cold water running down the back of my neck. I thought I'd be here a matter of days. Not weeks or months or years.

The nurse walks past the end of my bed and back towards the door, closing it behind her. Moments later the lights overhead dim and eventually they're switched off altogether.

I close my eyes and try to fall back into the peaceful oblivion of sleep, but I'm too troubled by what Will just said. I can't ignore the fear that creeps up the back of my spine. What if I never leave this place?

CHAPTER THREE

A t 8 A.M. the lights are unceremoniously thrown on again. There is less groaning this time, mostly because some of the younger kids haven't been able to sleep since they were woken for their check ups earlier and have kept the rest of us awake.

There are no check ups now though. Instead, trays of food are brought in and placed on the small table attached to each bed.

I wrinkle my face with disgust when my meal arrives.

'Not a fan of porridge?' Will asks.

'It's the worst,' I respond. My stomach grumbles though, so I take a pained bite and slowly work my way through the gruel.

Will laughs at my expression as I take another mouthful. 'We have the same thing every morning.'

'You're kidding!'

'I wish I was.' He screws up his own face and takes a bite. 'I think this is even worse than the stuff they gave us in the ARC.'

'Probably,' I say.

'You'd think Joseph would be able to supply his hospital with something a little more appetising.'

'You'd think,' I respond, cautiously. I remember hearing Joseph's name before, and know he is the man in charge of Hope, but I didn't realise he also ran the hospital. I quickly move away from the subject, not wanting to sound too ignorant. 'Which ARC are you from?'

'Gemini,' he says. 'You?'

'Aquarius,' I reply, remembering the name Sophie and James had given the place when we met at school in East Hope.

'Ah,' he says, his eyes lighting up with recognition. 'Funny how some of them have star signs for names, considering it was something from the stars that screwed us over.'

'Mmm,' I agree.

'Building a series of fallout shelters and naming them after star signs is just asking for trouble from the heavens,' he continues, with a glance up at the ceiling as though he can see the stars that lie far beyond it.

He takes a saddened breath as he eyes his next spoonful of porridge. Instead of lifting it to his mouth, he moves his spoon around the bowl. 'Do you have family up here?' he asks.

'No, my family died on impact,' I respond, trying to avoid eye contact with him. 'I have a friend up here I'm looking for, well, was looking for. I guess that will have to wait now.' I try not to appear too worried about putting the search for Sebastian on pause, but the thought distresses me and Will seems to notice the concern in my eyes. I rush on before he can question me about it further. 'How about you?' I ask.

'No, no family up here. Everyone in the ward seems to be alone, with no parent or guardian on the surface. So, I guess you fit the bill.'

I glance around the room at the other occupants. 'They're all alone?' I ask, keeping my voice low.

He nods. 'At least, on the surface they are,' he replies.

I continue searching the faces around me. It's too much of a coincidence that everyone in here is without parents, but I'm not sure what it means.

LATER THAT MORNING, Will goes for a series of tests. I'm beginning to wonder if he even needs to breathe, the way he can talk for minutes on end without pausing for air. The room almost seems too quiet without him here.

I close my eyes and take a deep breath, slowly exhaling it out. Will said it could be days before I'm taken for another round of tests. I don't want to wait though, this place makes me nervous and I want to be out of here as soon as possible.

I feel a presence next to the bed and crack one eye open to find one of the younger girls with her face right up next to mine, staring at me.

I impulsively jerk back and gasp.

'Who are you?' she asks.

I slowly sit up in bed and try to calm my erratically beating heart. 'Hasn't anyone ever told you not to sneak up on people?'

The girl ignores my question and clambers onto my bed. 'I'm Kelsey,' she announces, as she crosses her legs. I recognise her as the child who'd been unabashedly watching me when I first entered the room last night. She's tiny, with a mop of long golden hair that reaches down to her waist, and bright blue eyes. She's looking at me in an incredibly serious way for someone so young. 'What's your name?'

'I'm Elle,' I respond.

'What are you doing here Elle?' she asks, crossing her arms over her chest. I want to smile at how serious she's being. It is incredibly cute. I don't want to give her the impression I'm not taking her questions seriously though. It seems important to her.

'I'm here like the rest of you, because I'm sick.'

Kelsey taps her chin with her fingers. 'Are you having the injections too?'

'Only blood tests so far,' I respond. 'Do you have injections?'

'Sometimes. But I only get a sweet if I'm really good and don't cry. I barely ever cry,' she says, with an assertive shake of the head.

Her eyes flicker over to Will's bed. 'Is Will your boyfriend?' she asks.

'What? No!'

She tilts her head as she watches me. 'Are you sure?'

'Extremely,' I respond. He's several years younger than me and I've only just met him. Not to mention, he's also a head shorter. I guess to someone so young she doesn't quite grasp that. Her small shoulders relax and I get the feeling she is a little bit in love with Will herself. 'Is he *your* boyfriend?' I ask.

She giggles and shakes her head. 'No.'

'I think he might be...'

The door opens and Will is wheeled back into the room. Kelsey giggles even harder and buries her face in my bed.

'What's so funny?' Will asks, as he stands from the wheelchair and walks towards us.

Kelsey's body shakes uncontrollably, as she tries to stop herself from laughing.

'Kelsey and I were just talking about you actually,' I say.

Kelsey's laughter stops and she sits up and looks at me, horrified.

'No we weren't,' she says.

'Weren't we?'

She shakes her head, her eyes pleading with me not to say a word.

'Hmm, my mistake.'

Will frowns, but then smiles and sits on the end of my bed next to her. She crawls onto his lap, looking extremely pleased with the situation.

'How did your treatment go?' I ask.

'It was okay, they had me doing a stress test today.'

'A stress test? Is that normal?'

He shrugs. 'It's the first one I've done.'

'What did you have to do?'

'They had all these wires attached to me and I was on a treadmill for a while. It wasn't bad.'

'That doesn't seem like the kind of thing they should be putting a sick person through, don't you think?'

'It was fine, really.'

I frown, but don't say another word, keeping my misgivings to myself. 'What do you guys exactly do all day everyday. You're not so sick you need to be in bed, and it must get pretty boring doing nothing.'

Will checks the time on his cuff. 'They'll be bringing a TV in soon with a bunch of movies we can watch. The little kids pretty much always decide what is picked though, so you better prepare yourself. I hope you like Disney films.'

Kelsey's eyes light up at the sound of Disney. 'Cinderella is my favourite,' she says. 'One day I'm going to lose a glass slipper and marry a prince.' She glances up at Will, before quickly looking away. I try to hide a smile, but can feel the corners of my mouth lifting.

'There are also board games in the corner of the room,' Will adds.

'Anything good?' I ask.

Will goes to respond, but Kelsey interrupts, squealing with delight as she launches herself from the bed and across the room towards a television set an orderly is wheeling in. She doesn't seem sick enough to be in a hospital ward for treatment. I wonder what could be wrong with her and if she's here for the same reason I am.

I let out an involuntary sigh as I watch her race over to the television with the other kids. I wish I knew how I came to be here. It seems strange I don't remember anything at all. It's like a thick fog has descended on my mind and I struggle to push through the haze to recall what happened.

When I focus, I am almost able to sense the memories through the mist, but they are as formless as the clouds that conceal them. Wisps of colour and vague blurry outlines briefly materialise through the fog, only to quickly disperse as though caught by a sudden gust of wind.

'Are you okay?' Will asks.

'Yeah, fine,' I reply, locking eyes with him and giving him a reassuring smile.

He frowns as he watches me closely. 'Are you sure? You seem worried.'

I glance over my shoulder at Kelsey who is chatting animatedly with one of the other girls, before turning back to him. 'I'm just trying to recall my memories. I don't remember anything about being brought here the night before last. The doctor said it was because of a sedative I was given, but I haven't begun to remember anything yet.'

'You don't remember anything at all?'

'Nothing. Not even a tiny bit,' I respond, biting down on my lower lip. 'I would've thought I'd have remembered *something* by now.'

'Why did you need a sedative?'

'He said I was having trouble sleeping, but I don't remember, of course. You didn't have a sedative?'

'No,' he replies. 'But I wouldn't stress. I'm sure the doctor is right and you will get your memories back.'

I shrug, not feeling certain of anything right now.

'How were your first round of tests yesterday?'

I cross my arms over my chest. 'Uncomfortable. I felt more like a lab rat than a patient, the way they stuck so many needles in me.'

Will's eyes light up. 'Nothing wrong with being a rat. Did you know they used to train rats to detect landmines?'

'No, I didn't,' I frown. 'It doesn't mean I want to be one though.'

He gives me a look like I'm crazy for not wanting to be a rat. 'I suppose.'

He moves off the end of my bed, standing and stretching his arms over his head as he watches the orderly who is in the process of setting up the television for the younger kids. The man has a massive grin on his face as he chats to the kids about movie options, but there's an air of falseness to his behaviour that bothers me.

The guy strikes me as weirdly familiar, though I've never seen him before, and a bad feeling forms in the pit of my stomach. My attention is snatched away from watching the man as Will staggers back against my bed, causing the metal frame to rattle as he grabs it for support.

I jump up to help steady him and take a hold of his arm. 'Are you okay?'

He doesn't respond immediately, his eyes are wide with shock and his face has paled significantly. The grip he holds on the bed frame tightens as he considers the distance between our two beds, as if wondering whether he can manage the few steps across.

'Will?'

'I'm fine. Just got up a little too quickly,' he replies, with a nervous chuckle. There's an edge of worry to his voice and he eyes the ground beneath his feet with distrust. It's several moments before he straightens his back and allows me to help him to his bed. I watch him closely even after he's safely tucked under the sheets.

What if he's worse than I'd first assumed? I glance around the rest of the room, seeing the kids in here more clearly than I had before. What if we all are?

I swallow and try to take a calming breath as I return to my bed. I'm in a room of sick, possibly dying, kids and I am one of them. There may be no coming back from this.

CHAPTER FOUR

I sit in silence, allowing my thoughts to readjust, as I try to accept the new reality of my life. I want to remain positive, to have faith everything will be okay, but darkness invades my mind. My thoughts turn despondent as I consider the possibility that each person in this room has an expiry date, and the doctors here are our only hope of survival.

I hazard a glance at Will, whose eyes are just as concerned as my own. The colour is back in his cheeks and he appears to be feeling fine now. Maybe the stumble really was just a result of standing too quickly?

My troubled thoughts consume me as the afternoon wears on. I can barely bring myself to join in conversation with Will. Even Kelsey, with her unbridled enthusiasm for life, struggles to draw a smile from my face.

It's not until I wake up in the middle of the night, sweating and gasping for air, that I am roused from the melancholy that had descended upon me.

The ward is dark and long black shadows rear up in the dim light of the room. Gripped in the powerful and consuming terror of my nightmare, it takes me several moments to remember where I am. I try to calm myself from the fear that cloaks me like a cold and icy blanket.

I push myself up in bed and hug my knees to my chest as I draw in a long and deep breath. The dream was terrifyingly real. I can still feel its dark tendrils enclosing me, like long coils of a plant that creep up my back and curl around my neck and arms. I flick on the soft night light next to my bed and take another calming breath in and out.

'It was just a dream.'

Even whispering the words out loud doesn't calm me the way it should. I replay the dream in my mind, over and over, the images still as crystal clear in my thoughts as they had been in my sleep.

I was in a room; similar to the isolated one I awoke in just two mornings ago. There were no tables or chairs in there and the harsh white light that shone down on me was intense and ceaseless. I sat alone on the hard concrete floor, curled up and whimpering. It felt like I'd been in there for an eternity. My bones ached and my muscles felt weak. My throat was bone dry like I hadn't had a drink in days.

'Try again,' a voice boomed over a speaker. The sound sent shivers down my spine and a dark premonition filled me. I knew something bad was coming. I was certain of it, and yet I looked up at the ceiling from where the noise had sounded and shook my head.

'You can't make me,' I replied, wiping one hand across my tear-stained cheek and looking directly into the eye of a camera that was lodged in the corner of the room.

Silence met my words and the foreboding fear that had been building inside me rapidly escalated. I knew with a cold certainty things were about to get worse for me.

The door to the room slammed open and I crawled backward, weakly dragging my body until I was up against the far wall. My heart raced as the orderly I'd seen earlier today in the children's ward entered the room. He didn't approach me; he barely spared a glance in my direction. He merely stood back as he waited for the dark presence that stood just outside the doorway to enter.

I couldn't see the face of the man who stood outside the room. He was totally cloaked in shadow and, seeing him there, my body pulsed with a mixture of terror and fear of what was to come. My skin buzzed as though electricity danced over the tips of the hairs on my arms.

'Try again,' the voice over the speaker repeated.

I shook my head once more, too terrified to voice my refusal, but too determined to give in. I wouldn't give them what they wanted. I didn't even know if I could.

The shadowed man entered the room; his face was still shrouded in darkness. Even under the bright light that shone down from the ceiling I was unable to make out his features.

'I will ask you one more time Elle...' the voice rumbled. 'You know what's at stake here.'

'No,' I whispered, refusing to look away from the dark man who stood before me.

The voice over the microphone paused, before exhaling. 'Do it,' it said, with detached resignation. The words clearly not meant for me.

The man took another step towards me. Moments later my head erupted in pure, searing pain, like a burning poker had been plunged into my brain. I grabbed my head in my hands and screamed, the terror and agony too much for me to bear, even while asleep. When my eyes next opened I was back in the children's ward, my head still throbbing and my heart thundering in my chest.

'It was just a dream,' I repeat to myself.

I try to return to sleep, but the thought of sleeping makes me nervous, and I fear drifting back to my dream and seeing it through to completion. I can too easily recollect the intense pain in my head and I'm petrified of seeing the face of the man masked in shadow. I know it's just a dream, but it felt so real. As I lie in the darkened room, I can't quite convince myself to forget about it the way I would during the day.

In the end I give up on sleep and grab a book from the bookshelf at the end of the room. The feel of the paper in my fingers and the words enveloping me from the page are calming and by the time everyone's up for breakfast the next morning, I feel better. Well, almost. My eyes feel like sandpaper and I'm uncontrollably yawning, but the dream seems to be becoming more fiction-like and something only to be feared in the middle of the night.

After breakfast, whilst a nurse is clearing away our trays, I notice Kelsey approaching the lady. She tugs on the woman's skirt, causing her to pause what she is doing and give the small child her attention. Kelsey gives a theatrical sigh. 'Porridge is ruining my life,' she announces seriously, causing me to laugh out loud.

The nurse shoos her off as she continues to wheel the food trays from the room. I can't keep the smile from my lips. I kind of wish the nurse had at least listened to her; porridge is ruining my life too.

Once the door has shut behind the nurse, Kelsey turns and notices me watching. She smiles and makes her way over to my bed, her eyes latching onto the book in my hands as she approaches. 'What's that?' she asks, tilting her head to look at the cover. I wedge one finger between the pages I have open and flip the book to look at the front of it.

'The Lion, the Witch and the Wardrobe,' I answer, with a smile. 'It's about some children who find a magical land with talking animals in their wardrobe.'

Her eyes light up. 'Can you read some to me?' she asks.

I fold the corner of the page I'm on and close the book. 'Yeah, I'd be happy to, but maybe later. I might become cross-eyed if I read anymore right now.'

'How about we play a board game?' Will asks, coming to join us on the bed.

'I want to do a puzzle,' Kelsey says, racing off to the shelves at the end of the room, before we have a chance to respond. I smile as I watch her go, loving how enthusiastic she is and how little this place seems to affect her.

'Did you get any sleep last night?' Will asks.

'Not really.' I cross my arms over my chest to fight the chills that creep down my back, as my dream from last night rises to the surface of my thoughts. I can almost feel the residual pain in my mind, like my brain is scarred from the short moments of agony I was put through just before I woke up. I still can't get past how clear the dream was. It's unnerving.

'I got it,' Kelsey says, walking back with the puzzle in hand. She is nearly to the bed when she pauses, her grip on the tattered box tightening and her skin going pale.

Her eyes lose focus and a sheen of sweat develops on her forehead.

'Kels?' Will asks, standing and then crouching beside her. 'What's the matter?'

The box slowly tumbles from her grasp, hitting the ground with a clatter, sending the puzzle pieces tumbling across the floor. Kelsey's lower lip trembles and she raises her hands to grip her head in pain.

'I don't feel so good,' she whimpers, before collapsing into his arms, as a slow trickle of blood oozes out of one of her nostrils.

CHAPTER FIVE

I reach up and slam my fist against the bright red emergency button on the wall. Will's head whips up from Kelsey's limp body held in his arms to look at me, his wide eyes brimming with terror.

'What's wrong with her?' I ask, throwing myself from the bed to crouch down beside him.

'I don't know. She was fine a minute ago...'

'Kelsey, are you alright?' I ask, gently shaking her shoulders. 'Can you hear me?'

Her eyes stay shut and she doesn't respond. I place my cheek down close to her mouth, before pulling back. 'She's still breathing.'

'Will she be okay? Her skin is so pale,' Will says, pushing a stray strand of hair from across her face.

'I have no idea. Let's get her to a bed,' I suggest. Will nods and together we lift and place her on his bed. Her skin burns hot under my hands and her thin nightgown clings to the sweat coating her body.

The door at the far end of the room stays shut and there's no sign anyone has even heard our emergency call, let alone that they're responding to it.

'Where are the doctors?' I ask.

'I don't know. They should be here by now...'

The door at the end of the room slams open and the nurse on duty hurries in. She's in such a rush she doesn't close the door behind her and for the briefest moment I consider the open doorway and the escape it offers. I quickly shake my head and focus back on Kelsey.

'What happened?' the nurse asks, as she moves to Kelsey's side.

'She just collapsed,' I reply. 'She's still breathing, but she won't respond.'

'And her nose started bleeding,' Will adds. 'Is she going to be alright?'

'I need you both to step back,' the nurse responds, without so much as a glance our way. She grabs Kelsey's wrist with two finger-tips and falls silent.

'Why wasn't someone called sooner?' she says, after a minute.

'It only just happened!'

'She seemed fine just before!'

The nurse lifts the rails from the side of the bed, clicking them into place on either side of it. She moves purposefully and without hesitation. There's a grim set to her lips that makes me worry about how grave Kelsey's situation is.

'Where are you taking her?' Will asks, stepping forward as the woman pushes the bed out from the wall.

She ignores Will, instead lifting her CommuCuff to her lips. 'Dr. Milton, we have a code pink. I'm bringing her to you now.' She lowers her wrist and uses both hands to move the bed more swiftly towards the door.

'What's a code pink?' I ask, following the woman. The other kids all hang back silently, their eyes glued on Kelsey as the woman pushes her bed down the aisle between the other beds.

'Will she be okay?' I persist, when she doesn't respond.

The nurse's gaze refuses to move from Kelsey and the door she is headed for. She continues forward without answering me. When she nears the door at the end of the room I catch sight of a man in a black recruiter's uniform standing on the other side.

I don't have a chance to get a proper look at the man, as within a matter of moments Kelsey disappears from view and the door is slammed shut after her. I sink down onto the cold tiled floor, clutching my knees to my chest, feeling suddenly exhausted.

'How did she become sick so quickly?' I ask, as Will lowers himself to sit beside me. 'How is it fair?'

'It's not,' he replies.

I lower my head onto the tops of my knees and stare up at the door Kelsey disappeared through. It's wider than your average door and has shiny metal doorknobs and a slick black security pad on the wall next to it. My mind wills it to reopen and for Kelsey to return, but of course it doesn't.

I look down at my fingers and slowly scratch at the skin around my nails. 'Do you think she will recover?'

Will doesn't respond, so I glance at him. His teeth chew so angrily on his lower lip it's started to bleed and his eyes, which are normally so blue, seem darker.

I lean back and turn my body to face him. 'Have you seen this happen before?' I continue.

His gaze flicks to meet mine for a brief moment before settling back on the door. I'm shocked by the degree of pain I see in them. 'Just once,' he says.

'And?'

He lowers his head. 'And the kid never came back.'

I reach over and lightly touch his arm. 'That doesn't mean the same thing will happen to her. I only met her briefly, but she's got a lot of fight in her. She will be fine.' My words sound certain, and thankfully don't betray the doubt I feel inside.

He gives me a fleeting smile. 'I hope so. She's one of the good ones.'

We fall into a tense silence, each of us trying not to worry about

Kelsey but failing badly. Almost an hour later, the doorknob moves and I'm on my feet before my brain has a chance to register the movement. My heart has leapt with me and sits at the base of my throat, pounding quickly as I wait for it to open.

'Kelsey?' Will asks, having stood just as quickly.

The same orderly from my dream last night enters, pushing a television into the room. 'Who's ready to watch a movie?' he asks, attempting to inject enthusiasm into his voice..

Some of the younger children squeal with delight, and rush over to the screen. I freeze at the sight of him and eye the man closely. I feel an immediate and intense distrust for him. I try to shake the feeling off, but remembering him being in my dream last night makes me shiver. I take a step closer to him.

'What are you doing?' Will asks, eyeing me like I've grown a second head as I move to follow the younger kids.

'I'm not watching the movie. I just want to ask the guy about Kelsey.'

Will shakes his head. 'Good luck with that,' he responds, lowering himself back to the ground.

I ignore his comment and walk over to the man, my wariness for him only increasing as I approach. His dark eyes are slightly too far apart and with a short nose and narrow nostrils, he looks a bit like a snake.

I wait off to the side, while he finishes setting the movie up. Once it's playing he retreats to the door, but I head him off before he can reach it.

'The girl who was just taken from here, Kelsey, can you tell us what's happened to her?' I ask.

His eyes widen when he sees me and he avoids meeting my gaze as he shakes his head. 'Sorry, but I haven't heard anything about that.' He tries to move past me, but I move in time with him to block his way.

'Surely you can find out?'

He keeps his eyes focused on the door. 'You don't need to worry, the girl is in good hands.' He gives me a brief look and smiles for effect, but the smile is as empty as his words.

'I'm sure she is, but we're all worried. Can't you find out for us if she's okay?'

'No, I can't. They'll bring her back once she's recovered.'

I reach out and grab his arm, to stop him from leaving. 'When will that be?'

He shakes my hand from his arm. 'Once she's recovered,' he repeats. 'Excuse me.'

He shoves past me, not even trying to be gentle as he moves to get by. I stumble back several steps, seething as I watch him leave. His movements are hurried and he doesn't look back once as he escapes.

My shoulders sag as the door clicks shut. I feel a lot of my fight going out of me and I return to sit on the ground by Will.

'So?' Will asks.

'No luck,' I say, as I make myself comfortable on the floor. 'Do you know what Kelsey's diagnosis is?'

'Same as everyone else, her cells are mutating too fast.'

I pause. 'But they told me not everyone in here had the same diagnosis.'

'Are you sure that's what they told you?'

'Yeah.'

'Well, ask anyone in here, they'll all tell you they have the same thing. Maybe you misheard them?'

I frown. 'Maybe,' I say, but I'm not convinced.

When the movie finishes the snake-like orderly from earlier comes back with a nurse in tow. The man hurriedly moves towards the screen, taking care not to look anywhere but directly at it. The other woman walks in our direction.

'What's she here for?' I whisper to Will.

'No idea, they've already taken all the kids who are having tests today. Hopefully she's here to tell us about Kelsey?'

35

I frown and face the woman again. Her eyes meet mine, and something about the way she looks at me causes my blood to run cold. 'They don't take kids for tests later in the day?' I ask.

'Never,' he replies. 'Why?'

'Because I think she's here for me.'

CHAPTER SIX

The nurse moves through the room with purpose and her gaze doesn't shift from mine as she continues down past the other beds heading directly for us; the cold certainty I felt moments ago getting stronger with each step she takes. There is something in the way the woman looks at me that makes my heart beat a little quicker.

'She can't be here for you,' Will says, glancing at the nurse before settling his gaze back on me. There's complete certainty in his voice and he doesn't for a second entertain the possibility. Everything in this place runs to a strict schedule and in Will's mind the tests are always finished by this time in the day. Even just a couple of nights in here have shown me that.

Her feet stop directly in front of us. 'Elle, it's time for your treatment. Would you like me to bring a chair for you?'

'No,' I respond, standing. 'I'm okay.'

Will tugs on the leg of my pants as I stand to follow the woman. 'This isn't normal,' he whispers. It's not surprising Will would be freaked by a change to the schedule, especially after what happened to Kelsey today.

I raise my hands and shrug. 'It will be fine,' I murmur back. I don't feel particularly comfortable with the situation, but even if it wasn't fine, there's nothing I can do and worrying Will won't help.

The nurse takes me out of the ward and down through several corridors before she stops by one of the rooms. She bumps her cuff against the scanner by the door and reaches for the handle. She is just about to turn it when I hear footsteps down the far end of the corridor.

A man being pushed in a wheelchair appears. At least, I think it's a man. I push down a gasp as I get a better look at him. The skin all over his body is raised and calloused, with large bleeding scabs peeling off of him. The decaying flesh is sickly, it's almost the colour of stone, and you can barely see his eyes beneath his large and mottled forehead that hangs low over them.

I take an unconscious step towards him to get a closer look, but the nurse grabs my arm and quickly ushers me into the room, closing the door firmly shut behind us.

'Who was that?' I ask her.

She avoids my gaze. 'You shouldn't have seen him,' she mutters.

'Is he being treated here?' I continue. 'What's wrong with him?'

'Not all talents are things to be envied,' she says, almost more to herself than in answer to my question. She turns and moves away from the door. 'Just this way.' She waves for me to follow her.

The room is almost identical to the one I'd been in last night. Metal counters line the walls, covered in an array of different machines. Down the centre of the room is a long table, its surface empty of any clutter.

'Am I having more blood tests?' I ask the woman.

'Not today.' I want to be relieved, but the tone of her voice stirs the unease in my gut. Am I about to receive something worse?

She leads me past the benches and through a door at the other end of the room. She clicks the door shut behind me and I peer around the small space we've entered. It's darker in here, with less equipment than the room we just walked through and a reclining chair in the centre. The chair is similar to one you'd sit in when getting your teeth checked, which causes my curiosity to spike.

'Can you take a seat for me?' the nurse asks.

I move over to the chair, but stop before getting on, lightly running my fingers over the arm rests.

'Is this a part of my treatment?' I ask.

'Yes.'

The door opens behind the woman and a man in a recruiter's uniform enters. He has an imposing figure with shoulders that take up most of the doorframe. His lips form a straight line and the way his eyes fall on me causes me to unconsciously take a step closer to the chair.

I swallow and look back to the nurse as the man shuts the door behind him. 'What am I having done today?' I ask her.

'The doctor will explain when he arrives. Please take a seat.'

I hesitate, the treatment can't be good if they've sent muscle in here to watch, but one look from the man in black and I take my seat on the chair, clasping the armrests tightly as I wait.

I try to catch the nurse's eye as she goes about preparing the room, in an attempt to gauge any idea of what's to come, but she avoids looking at me to the point where I feel certain it's on purpose.

When the door opens again a tall man in a white lab coat enters the room. His shoulders are hunched and his focus is entirely on the tablet he holds, so much so he nearly falls over his feet while trying to close the door behind him.

Glancing up at the nurse he gives a curt nod, before focusing back on the tablet. The nurse approaches a screen that is attached to the chair and moments later the seat begins to recline. My body stiffens and I clasp the arms of the chair tightly.

'What's happening?' I ask her.

Again, my question is met with silence and her eyes refuse to meet mine. The unease I've been feeling since entering the room increases and, though I try to stay calm, my gut warns me something with this situation is wrong.

The doctor approaches the bench and I roll my head to look at him, trying my best to ignore the commanding figure of the recruiter who scowls at me from behind. 'What am I having done today?' I try to sound firm and confident, but my voice squeaks as the words come out.

I hear the distinct ripping of Velcro and when I look down I find the nurse and recruiter placing restraints over each of my wrists. I immediately sit up.

'What are you doing?' I attempt to pull my hands back, but the restraints are tightened before I get a chance. I push my wrists against the straps trying to get out from under them, the movement only becoming more agitated as I fail to get my hands loose.

'Are these necessary?' I ask.

The woman takes a quick step back from the chair. 'You need to calm down Elle,' she says.

Already my wrists feel chafed from rubbing against the material, but this doesn't stop my attempts to get free. 'I'll calm down when I'm not being tied down. Take them off!'

'Doctor?' the nurse asks.

A set of wide hands grab my shoulders, wrenching me back to lie in the chair. I catch sight of the recruiter's scowl as he pushes me down, but it doesn't still me. If anything, it makes me fight harder.

'Get your hands off me!' I yell, fighting to sit up again. The man's hands are steadfast though and don't budge even slightly, despite the way I try to throw myself forward as I attempt to get free.

The nurse quickly tightens a restraint over my ankles, legs and chest, effectively stopping my struggles. The thick bands dig uncomfortably into my skin and there is no room for movement beneath them.

She moves closer to my head, and there's another sound of ripping Velcro before she places one last restraint over my forehead, stripping all movement from me completely.

My breathing becomes erratic as I realise my fight against the thick fastenings tightened across my body is completely useless. There's no escaping. I'm trapped.

I can feel a tear running down my cheek and another one joins it as I realise I'm unable to even wipe it away. 'What are you doing to me?'

'Calm down Elle,' the doctor says. 'We're going to do an eye examination. The restraints are merely to make sure you don't move during the procedure. It won't hurt a bit.'

It's a lie of course. Adults only ever say it won't hurt when it most definitely will. Why else would I need to be strapped down to the table with a recruiter here to make sure I comply?

A bright light is switched on overhead, momentarily blinding me. The doctor leans over, tilting the light so it is no longer haloed behind his head and instead focuses in on me from an angle.

He pulls back and when he returns he forces my eyelids open to squeeze drops of liquid into my eyes.

'Can you close your eyes for me Elle?'

I do as he says, feeling even more vulnerable now my eyes are shut. My hands grip the arms of the chair tightly, my nails digging into the hard leather, and I nervously chew on the inside of my lip.

'Now, open them.'

I slowly blink my eyes open. The doctor's face is mere inches from mine and I can feel his rancid breath against my cheek.

'Look to the left,' he says. 'And now the right.'

He readjusts the light again. 'That's great Elle. Now I can begin.' Though he sounds calm and professional, the way he says, 'begin,' causes me to shudder.

A metal device appears in his hand and I jerk back against the chair, the restraints biting keenly into my skin. He holds the device calmly in one hand and as he moves it closer the light dances along its cool metal tongs. I eye the two large scoop like ends with total fear. It looks like some sort of clamp and I have a sickening certainty of what he's about to cinch open with it. My heart races and I can feel adrenaline rushing through my system in response.

'What are you doing with that?' My lips quiver and my breath comes faster.

'I will just put this in your eyes to keep them open. The area is anesthetised so you won't feel a thing.'

'What?' I jerk back against the chair again, fighting against the restraints. 'I don't want this. Please don't do this.'

'Elle you need to calm down. If you don't stay perfectly still this will hurt.'

I want to calm at his words, but they only make me more agitated. 'Please don't do this!'

The man doesn't listen though and I watch in terror, unable to do anything to stop him, as he lowers the clamps down and peels back my upper and lower eyelid with the device on one eye, then the other.

I'm surprised not to feel pain, only an uncomfortable pressure, but this hardly helps my concerns when he lowers a metallic ring down onto my eyes that immobilises them completely.

'Please,' I cry out, desperately hoping he will change his mind, but he ducks away out of sight. I am left with only the bright light above me for company, and even that has become blurry.

When the doctor's face returns, a long needle also comes into view with a bright purple serum inside the tube.

'No,' I whimper, already coming to the undeniable conclusion he plans to put that thing in my eye. 'Surely there's another way.'

'Now you'll probably feel a little pinch.' He lowers the needle closer and closer towards my eye. I want to fight against my restraints, to pull away in terror, but I'm completely frozen as he carefully places the needle against my right eye and slowly pushes into it.

I groan in discomfort at what's being done. At first, I barely feel the needle and it is merely uncomfortable. But then comes a sharp, stinging pain as he slowly injects the serum.

I forget to breathe as the sting continues, gritting my teeth as I wait for the pain to subside. But there is no end to it and when it all becomes too much I scream out in agony.

The injection takes minutes, though it feels like an eternity. I desperately want to pass out and escape from the searing pain, but there is no getting away from it.

When he finally removes the needle, I am breathless and sagging into the chair.

'Please don't do that again,' I whisper.

He disappears from view and reappears with another needle in hand. I make a tiny groaning noise, dreading what I know will come next.

'Please—' my begging is cut off as another scream rips from my throat.

CHAPTER SEVEN

'**S**he shouldn't still be asleep. Should she?' a woman whispers. Her voice is muffled like she's speaking from another room, but I hear her words surprisingly clear.

I groan softly and open my eyes but immediately wish I hadn't. Pain shoots through them as they open and they feel like they're on fire. The room is too bright and my vision is completely blurred. I struggle to even see the large lamp that hangs above my head. The edges of it are indistinct and the light it emanates smudges into the space around it.

I lift my hand above my head to look at it, before dropping it quickly away. I can barely make out my fingers.

What did they do to me?

I close my eyes and take a slow, uneven breath. Why can I barely see the shape of my hand, let alone any detail? Why do my eyes feel like they're about to burst into flame?

I run my hands along the armrests, the warm leather feeling reassuring against my skin until my fingers skim across the thick Velcro straps that were used to tie me down. My fingers freeze before drawing away. At least the restraints have been removed.

'She should be awake at any time now,' a man replies. The door dampens the sound, but I still manage to catch his words, which almost seem to faintly echo off the hard surfaces in the room next door.

'And the procedure?'

'I believe it was a success, but I won't be able to test the results for a few days.'

'Do we need to turn up the inhibitor sensors?' the woman asks.

'No, she's doped up on sedatives right now and should be fine until she reaches the ones in the children's ward.'

There are footsteps and then the squeak of a doorhandle turning.

'Doctor?' the woman asks, as the movement of the handle pauses. 'Do you think she will survive this?'

My body stills and my breathing stops as I lean closer to the door to hear his response.

'She's lasted six weeks of intense daily experiments, I don't see why not.'

I feel the colour drain from my face and the blood that runs through my veins turns cold. Six weeks of experiments? What is he talking about? Surely they can't mean me.

'Ah, you're awake,' the doctor says, as he pushes the door open. 'How do you feel?'

I shrink back, tumbling off the chair and moving to press myself against the far wall. My heart thunders in my chest, my terror made all the worse by my inability to see clearly.

'Why can't I see anything?' I ask.

'That can be a side effect of the procedure. You should be back to normal soon. Why don't you come and sit back in the chair?'

I shake my head vehemently and continue to claw my way along the wall, as I follow his slow, blurry movement towards me. He continues to draw closer and I am just able to make out his hands, which he raises to hold before him as though he were cautiously approaching a wild beast.

'Elle, will you please take a seat? I don't want you hurting yourself.'

I stumble into a small metal table causing the items on the tray on top to clatter. My mind is overwhelmed by what I overheard and though the clash of metal objects is as loud as a gong going off in my ear, I barely register the noise. Have I really been here so long? Why can't I remember anything? What have they been doing to me?

I swallow and attempt to take a steadying breath. I need to stay calm and give myself time to process what I've heard. It's hard to ignore the effect his words have had on me though. It's like they've resonated with a part of me deep down, and I know I can't trust these people.

'Would you fetch another sedative?' the doctor murmurs, under his breath to the nurse.

'Please don't,' I whimper. 'I just want to return to the ward.'

The doctor clears his throat and pauses before he answers. 'If you take a seat we won't need to administer a sedative.' There's a hint of surprise in his voice, as though he hadn't expected me to hear his whispers to the nurse. They'd been spoken so clearly though, I'm surprised he thought he was being discreet.

'Not in *that* chair,' I say, nodding my head in the direction of the chair I'd been tied to. I refuse to go anywhere near that thing again.

'No. We can bring a wheelchair in. Would that be okay?' He talks slowly and his words make me feel like I'm a small child, but I feel so vulnerable right now that his tone is welcome.

I nod and, as I do, the room flickers into focus. I see the doctor clearly, though the room around him stays blurred. Certain details seem to draw my attention and I find myself captivated by the clarity with which I see them. His worried eyes are deep blue and have touches of green flickered throughout them. His nose is dotted with large pores and there are a few tiny droplets of sweat above his upper lip.

My vision slips out of focus again as quickly as it came in and I stagger back against the wall.

I hear the doctor rush forward several steps. 'Please, take my arm,' he urges, holding it out to me.

I reach out and grasp onto his outstretched arm, using it to guide me to the wheelchair waiting by the door.

'Will you take me to the ward now?' I ask, my voice with a pleading edge to it.

'Yes, the nurse will take you in just one moment.'

He helps lower me to the chair and as he moves to take a step back I reach out and grab his arm, causing him to pause. 'Why?' I whisper to him.

'Why what?' he replies.

There are many 'whys,' I want answered, but only one I should utter aloud. 'The procedure. Why did I have to have it?'

'To make you better,' he responds, the tone of his voice changing as he utters the word, 'better.' He almost caresses the word. 'You should get some rest.' He easily moves out of my grasp, leaving me alone with the nurse.

My heart sinks as she wheels me from the room and my world continues to stay blurry. It's even more intimidating once we're in the corridor and the space moves by me in a bright, white blur.

My focus doesn't linger on my troubled vision though, as the other thoughts that fight for my attention rise to the surface of my mind.

Have I been here for six weeks? What experiments have they done on me? Why can't I remember them? When the nurse wheels me into the ward, the general hubbub of kids talking disappears and the room falls silent. Not so much as a whisper is heard as the wheelchair slowly rolls down the aisle between the beds, and my skin crawls as I feel eyes watching me go by.

'Is it that bad?' I ask Will, once the nurse moves away after helping me into bed. I try to focus on him, but all I can see is his blurry figure sitting up in bed. I strain my eyes in an attempt to see him clearly, desperate to see his reaction to how I look, but it hurts and I don't manage even a moment of clarity.

'Is what that bad?' he asks, lightly.

'My eyes,' I reply. 'Do they look bad?'

'Totally fine,' he lies, not missing a beat.

I raise one eyebrow at him. 'You don't need to lie. You know I can handle the truth.'

He pauses. 'Well, they may be a little bloodshot and a little puffy around the rims, but I'm sure it will pass. What treatment did they give you?'

'You don't want to know.' I draw my knees up into my arms and cuddle them close to my chest. The treatment is the least of my worries right now. I need to find out what happened to the last six weeks of my life and, after the treatment I received today, it's clear I need to find out fast. I'm not sure I want to be around to discover what they have planned for me next.

CHAPTER EIGHT

I t takes several days for the blurriness to subside and my vision
to completely clear. I've never felt sick like that before and
those first few hours after the treatment were brutal. I spent
most of them with my head in a bucket fighting uncontrollable waves
of queasiness and trying to ignore my incredibly itchy eyes. Will was
kind to me, making sure I had enough water and rubbing my back
when it all became too much.

There were times when my vision stayed blurry and others when
it became intensely clear. After struggling to see anything at all, the
moments of clarity were downright disturbing.

The troubles with my vision were nothing compared to the pure
dread I still feel about being called for another treatment and the
confusion I feel about what I overheard while in that room. I can't
bring myself to talk to Will about the details of what happened
though. Not yet at least.

'Can I tell you my random fact of the day?' Will asks.

I raise my head to look at him. His eyes are bright and he looks
desperate to tell me this one. He's been struggling to find energy for

even the simplest tasks today, so it's nice to see him excited about something.

'You know you want to hear it,' he says. 'Plus, it may just make you love rats even more.'

'Even more than you do?'

He grins. 'Well, that's impossible.'

'That must've been some pet you had back in the ARC,' I say, returning his grin. 'Okay, let me have it.'

The smile on his face widens. 'Rats can fall five stories and survive.'

'Really?'

'Yep.' He nods, proudly.

'What did you do to that poor rat?' I laugh.

His face drops and he gasps. 'I would never...'

'Kidding, kidding.' I smile and lean back against the bed head to stare at the ceiling. There's a tiny scuff of black on it I hadn't noticed before. 'They are pretty impressive I'll give you that.'

'Yeah, they're survivors. I think that's why I like them so much,' he replies.

I fall silent and lower my head to look down at my hands. I've lost weight since I've been here and the skin over my knuckles has tightened. The blue veins on the backs of my hands are more vivid than ever before and my fingers are always freezing cold. I'm surprised I hadn't noticed sooner.

Am I a survivor?

'Elle?'

'Mmm.'

'You don't have to tell me what happened in your treatment, but if you ever want to talk about it I'm happy to listen.'

'Thanks,' I reply, refusing to look at him. I can practically feel the sympathy in his eyes as he watches me. I don't need to see it.

The door at the end of the room opens and a nurse enters pushing the dinner trolley inside. She makes her rounds, dropping a tray at each bed and I sit up a little straighter as she nears mine.

'Any news of Kelsey?' I ask her, as she carries a tray of food to me from the trolley.

'I told you yesterday, and the day before, I can't give out other patient information.'

'Please?' Will asks.

The nurse shakes her head. 'I'm not able to give you an update.'

My shoulders sink and I lean back into bed as the woman continues to push her trolley down between the beds.

'I felt certain we'd get an answer that time,' Will says.

I play with my food with my fork. 'She's been gone for days. Why aren't they telling us anything?'

I hear Will swallow before he replies. 'I just hope she's okay,' he says.

The door at the end of the room opens and I glance over, curious as the nurse who brought us lunch is already in the room. A chair carrying a small, sleeping girl enters. Even though my sight has been far better, it takes me a moment to realise the girl is Kelsey.

'Will, Will!' I jump up from bed. 'It's Kelsey.'

His head whips up to look at her and he heaves himself from his bed, causing his food tray to drop on the ground. It lands with a crash, but he doesn't notice the food and cutlery rolling onto the floor.

'It's really her,' he says. 'But she looks different.'

We both clamber to get to her bedside as the nurse lifts her from the chair and places her into bed.

'Is she okay?' I ask him. She seems smaller than before and her skin is almost blue it's so pale. Her hair seems to have lost the richness to its colour and has become brittle and dry.

'I'm fine,' her small voice answers, before the nurse has a chance to respond.

'Hey Kels, how are you feeling?' Will asks, a massive grin on his face. He takes her hand and gives it a squeeze.

Her eyes slowly blink open. They look tired and the gutsy determination I noticed when I first met her is nowhere to be seen. She looks like a little girl who is extremely unwell and the sight scares me.

She's deteriorated so much in only a matter of days. Is this what happens to everyone in here?

I sneak a glance at Will. His health seems to have declined drastically during the short time I've known him. Even now, he's clawing onto his IV stand to keep himself upright. A sickening certainty enters the pit of my stomach. He's next.

'I'm fine,' she says, trying to sit up.

'You should rest,' I say, taking a seat on the bed by her side and propping pillows behind her back.

She pouts. 'But I want us to do a puzzle.'

'Maybe tomorrow,' I reply.

Will takes a seat on the other side of her bed. Relief fills his eyes now he no longer needs to stand. 'Where have you been the last few days?' Will asks.

'Nowhere,' Kelsey replies, frowning.

Wills eyes lock onto mine, before looking back at her. 'What do you mean, nowhere?' he asks.

Kelsey opens her mouth wide in a large yawn. Her eyes are already heavy with exhaustion, but she fights against sleep's pull.

'You kids should let her rest,' the nurse says.

I jump at his comment, not realising he was still at the end of her bed. I stand and take a step back. Will quickly follows, but we both continue to hover by her bedside.

Kelsey's breath has become steady and her eyes droop closer and closer to sleep. 'We'll see you in the morning,' I say, but I don't think she hears me, as she appears to have already drifted off.

'What did they do to her?' I ask Will, as we walk away.

'She's probably been sedated while they were treating her. Maybe she doesn't remember what happened over the last few days?'

'Maybe,' I reply. I also lost memories after being sedated though, and with six weeks of memories gone and lied about, it would be too convenient if Kelsey has lost hers too.

Will stumbles over his feet and I reach out to catch his arm, grasping it tightly, so as not to let go.

'Maybe I need some rest too,' he says, as he ever so slowly rights himself.

I don't respond. I can't. Seeing him looking so frail is frightening and makes my heart break. He was so much better when I first arrived, and seeing how quickly his illness has progressed in a matter of days is terrifying. He seems too exhausted to even notice it himself.

I help him over to his bed, only feeling my concern ease once he's safely under the covers. I stand back to look at him. He was fine until his last treatment, but since then he's only gotten worse.

'You feeling okay?' I ask.

He peers up at me, before rolling his eyes and snuggling his head back into the pillow. 'Stop looking at me like I'm dying.'

'I wasn't,' I try to object.

'Yeah, yeah. That's what they all say.' He softly laughs into his pillow.

I go to respond, but his breathing has already become heavy and there's a light wheeze to his breath. Instead, I slowly back away to my own bed.

He wasn't nearly this bad when I arrived. His bones were maybe showing more than they should and his skin was several shades paler than you'd expect, but he was fine. Why is he so much worse since his last treatment?

A sense of urgency stirs within me. I need to find out what is happening in this place. I need to know why these treatments are only making us worse. I try to settle down for the night, but I'm consumed by my worries and they stay with me as I fall into a broken and fitful sleep.

CHAPTER NINE

I bang my fist against the hard white door to my room. 'Will you let me out of here?' I scream. My voice sounds hoarse and disjointed, it almost echoes in the realm of my dream. I feel a desperate, consuming need to leave this place. 'You can't keep me in here forever!'

I beat my fist one last time against the door before collapsing down onto the floor and leaning my head against the cool tiles. I stare at a spot on the wall where there are notches that have been carved into it. There are five rows of five of the thin scratches. Only 25 days in here, but it feels like an eternity.

The dream fades out of focus, as though I'm waking up, but instead of returning to the darkness of the children's ward I am thrown back into the small lonely room. I'm lying on the small bed staring up at the ceiling. I hear movement out in the hallway and my eyes lift to the doorknob, waiting for it to turn. My heart beats quickly in my chest. I don't know what is coming, but I know when that door opens it's something to fear.

The doorknob twists and as the door swings in I see a familiar shadowed figure standing by the entrance to my room. He steps inside and I catch a brief glimpse of his face, but the shadows seem to follow him and quickly shroud him in darkness once again. From what I can see, he's not one of the doctors in here. Judging by the impeccable state of his navy-blue suit and his slicked back, gelled hair, he's someone important.

'What do you want?' I growl. 'You going to try and convince me you people want to help? I've already had the pep-talk.'

'Now, is that any way to treat a guest?' he asks, closing the door behind him. As the door shuts my dream ends and a thick fog blankets my thoughts. I try to push against the haze, desperate to see past it, but it's useless. My dream is trapped and I have no way to access it. As I slowly drift awake, I hear words in the recesses of my mind.

'If you agree to cooperate I will let you see the friend you were trying to escape North Hope with,' the man says.

My EYES fly open and my thoughts race as I try to process what I've dreamed ... or was it just a dream? It's the dead of night and all the children in the ward are asleep, but I couldn't feel more awake.

I keep repeating the words I'd heard as I floated back to consciousness. Was that the same shadowed man who haunted my sleep the other night? Who had he been talking about? What did he want me to do? I have so many questions, but I have no answers. Not yet.

Though the fragments of time I'd seen in sleep had been disjointed and confusing, they had also been incredibly clear. I feel like they couldn't be anything other than a memory, or maybe some sort of premonition? I desperately wanted to get out of the hospital in my dream and the need to leave easily resurfaces even now I'm awake. I can feel it resonating deep inside me, like a feeling recalled rather than something new.

I'm not exactly sure what the dream was, but resolve courses through my body and a steady certainty rushes through me. I have to trust my gut on this, and it's telling me this place isn't what it claims to be and we need to get out of here, fast.

WILL struggles to push himself into a seated position. 'They're taking you off for another round of treatment?' he asks.

I nod as I watch the woman re-enter the ward with a wheelchair for me. I hate having treatments, but after my dream last night I feel a sense of purpose to them. If I'm going to get us out of here, I need a plan and the first step is to find a way out of this building, which won't happen while I'm locked up inside this room.

'You've been getting them a lot,' Will says. 'I don't think you've had a day off this week.'

'Yeah, lucky me.' I try to keep my voice light, but the extra attention I've been getting can't be good. After each treatment I get seriously bad headaches and am in a constant state of queasiness. At least I can be grateful I haven't had anything too traumatic after the eye procedure.

'Well, don't have too much fun without me,' I joke to Will, when the nurse approaches the end of my bed.

Will gives me a smile. 'I won't.' The smile falls from his face and he coughs.

'You alright?' I ask.

'I'm fine. Just an itchy throat,' he rasps, when the coughing subsides.

He's trying to play it off like it's nothing, but he can't hide the fear in his eyes. When he notices me watching, he smiles brightly in an attempt to prove he's okay. I'm not fooled, and the urge to get us out of here stirs within me again.

'If you say so,' I mumble.

The nurse wheels me out of the room and into the corridor beyond. There is no one out here and the place is as empty as usual.

I close my eyes as we continue on and take deep breaths. The wheels on the chair squeak with each rotation and I can't fight the shivers that work their way down my spine as I listen. I hate going for tests and not knowing what I'm about to be subjected to. The more I have, the more powerless I feel.

It scares me to think I've lost all autonomy over my body. Especially when I'm questioning the procedures they're putting me through.

The wheelchair slows as we approach one of the nameless doors. I have no idea where I've been brought. Given the route we've taken and the small table by the doorway, I don't think I've been here before, but I won't be certain until I'm taken inside.

'What am I having done today?' I ask, trying to keep my voice steady.

The nurse ignores my question and proceeds to take my cuff off, placing it on the table outside the room before opening the door and pushing me inside.

As I enter I find myself facing a massive machine that takes up half the room. The monstrous cylindrical thing is large and round with a gapping hole through the centre of it that emits a soft blue glow. There's a large glass window along one wall and I can see two doctors sitting at computers on the other side. In the shadows behind them stands a man in a smart looking suit. The reflection from the window makes it difficult to see his face though.

'Who's that man in the suit?' I ask the nurse.

She glances at the glass wall and immediately stands a little straighter, smoothing down the front of her dress with her hands.

'Just someone here to observe,' she replies, turning away from the glass and leaning in close to me as if hoping her words won't be overheard.

I raise one eyebrow at her. It's pretty obvious he's not 'just someone.' The way the nurse's behaviour has changed in the last thirty seconds, you'd swear we were in the presence of royalty.

'Now, up onto the table with you,' she says, pointing at a long slab that extends from the mouth of the machine. I glance back at the glass to try and get a better look at the man, but he's standing too far away to see him clearly. I focus back on the task at hand.

'What is this?' I ask the nurse, eyeing the machine with distrust.

'It's an MRI scanner,' she replies. 'It will scan your body and take pictures of the inside.'

I scrunch my lips up as I consider the cold and intimidating machine. The sheer size of it is the stuff of nightmares. But, if it's just taking pictures, surely it can't be that bad.

The nurse helps me transfer onto the table and then injects a solution into my cannula. I rub at my face tiredly. I wish I'd been able to sleep better last night, but after waking from my dream Will's coughing kept me up. His breathing was so laboured I was scared he'd stop breathing all together if I fell asleep.

I know I've only just met Will, but I already feel close to him. I guess being in the hospital together does that. He's like a little brother to me and I want to protect him in any way I can.

The nurse has me lie back and she lowers a large cage down over my face. I shiver as she clips it shut, feeling a sudden wave of unease. The table slowly begins to move. It creeps its way into the large gaping mouth of the machine. Each inch it travels makes me more and more uncomfortable.

Like I've been swallowed and lie in the tight belly of a mechanical beast, the inside of the machine is uncomfortably narrow. A soft blue light illuminates the walls, though this does nothing to soothe my concerns about the confined space. It's small in here. *Really* small.

'Are you sure this is necessary?' I raise my voice to be heard beyond the walls of the machine, then pause, waiting for an answer, but no response comes. 'Hello?'

Again, my question is met with silence. I stare at the roof of the tunnel; trying to overcome my nerves I can feel tingling just below the surface of my skin. Why isn't the nurse answering me?

Deep breaths. I slowly count to distract myself, the numbers barely touching my lips as I breathe each one out. '*One, two, three...*'

'How are you doing in there Elle?' a man asks, over an intercom. I wince in reaction. The sound is loud and resonates along the walls of the tunnel making me feel surrounded by his voice.

Four, five, six...

'Elle?' he queries, when I fail to respond.

'Will this take long?' I ask, my voice sounding nervous even to my own ears. My hands are clammy and I feel as though a heavy weight presses down on my chest. This can't take long. I can't handle long in here.

'Not too long,' he answers. 'We need you to stay still while we take the pictures. Can you do that for me?'

'Yes,' I reply.

The speaker goes silent. Has it started? Is it nearly over? Am I meant to be still right now? The tunnel begins to feel smaller and I nervously tap my fingers on the table below me. This has to be over soon, surely.

'Okay, we're going to start now,' he says. 'Remember to stay perfectly still.'

I stop tapping my fingers, but I can still feel my nervous energy pulsing through them. I desperately want to crawl out of the tunnel, but I know they'll only make me do it again if I attempt to leave. I blow a slow breath out. It feels hot in here and the air around me seems thick and heavy.

This won't take long, I remind myself.

The machine roars to life and chugs loudly as it starts. I gasp in surprise. The noise is constant and fills the tunnel with its rumble. My nerves had been on edge before, but now I can feel my total fear of this machine rushing through my body.

I try to remember to count, to breathe, to do anything that will stop me from freaking out in here, but none of my usual tricks seems to work. All logic disappears and I am engulfed in a desperate need to get out of this machine.

The edges of my vision grow dark and I struggle to keep my arms by my side, my thoughts are entirely focused on pulling myself from my coffin-like surrounds.

The noise dies, leaving the tunnel eerily quiet.

'Is it over?' I ask, not knowing if anyone will hear me.

'Elle, you're doing really well. We will give you a few minutes to relax then we're going to take another set.'

My lips tremble and I fight back tears welling in my eyes.

'I can't do this,' I say. 'Please. It's too confined in here. I want to get out.'

The microphone goes silent.

When I don't hear a response I lift the mask from my face and push myself down along the table towards the opening.

'I can't do this,' I repeat.

'Elle?' the man asks. 'We need several more sets of scans, but if you can hold on for one more set we'll call it a day.'

'No. It's too hard.'

'If you would prefer we can give you a sedative to make you relax?'

I pause and try to give the logic in my brain a moment to override my body's determination to get out of here. I get the strong feeling if I leave the MRI scanner I will be getting a sedative whether I want one or not. I'd much rather just get this over with.

'Just one more set?' I ask, my hands already trembling at the thought.

'Just one more,' he confirms.

I force myself to shuffle back up the table and take my position. Every cell in my body screaming that I'm moving the wrong way, but I ignore the feeling and lay my arms flat by my sides as I wait for the process to begin again.

I take a steadying breath and focus on the soft blue light around me. I want to let it calm me, but my eyes keep flicking towards the opening at the end of the tunnel.

This is fine, I try to convince myself, determinedly moving my focus away from escape to the light that glows above. The machine makes a loud banging noise and the light flickers.

'What was that?' I ask, my words rushing out in a breath.

'Nothing to worry about. The light bulb in the machine probably needs chang—' The man's voice is cut off by feedback coming from the microphone. 'We're going to get started now.'

My hands ball up into fists. I want to shut my eyes and imagine I'm somewhere else, but I can't stop watching the tunnel walls. They feel like they're getting closer and closer.

The machine fires up again and my chest tightens, each loud chug making the space around me diminish. My throat constricts causing me to take short and painful gasps as I struggle to breathe.

The nervous energy in my fingertips travels up through my arms until they feel tingly. I slowly begin shaking as the energy pulses down through the rest of my body.

As convulsions grip me, a series of memories project in my mind. They filter through my thoughts quickly, as though each memory were a snapshot being flickered past my face. Hunter. We'd gone across the bridge together to the north. Sebastian. His face on seeing me again for the first time. His warmth hugging me like it used to. His revelation about my sickness, about his mum. Hunter gone. Sebastian disappearing. Recruiters. Darkness pulling me under. Then the white room. The endless time spent alone in the white room I woke in just a few weeks ago.

'Elle we need you to stay still,' the man booms, over the sound of the machine. But I can't stop the shudders that roll through me. My body is buzzing and my heartbeat races to keep up with it. I slam my hands against the sides of the tunnel as my body buckles and a scream rips from my throat. I get a powerful sting of an electric shock, which momentarily burns my hands then throws them back from the walls. The machine goes silent and the soft blue light disappears, plunging the tunnel into darkness.

I collapse back against the table, and the shaking that had moments ago consumed me is now completely gone. All that is left from the episode is a strange tingling in my fingertips, an over-whelming sense of exhaustion and my memories. I remember how I got here, though what happened once I arrived is still a little foggy.

The door to the room slams open.

'What happened?' a woman whispers. I stop breathing as I strain to hear her words.

'She shorted the circuit,' the man spits back, quietly.

'What?'

'I knew I should have administered a sedative,' he mutters.

'What about the inhibitors?'

'They're lowered when the machine is on,' he replies, keeping his voice soft. 'They have to be or we can't get a proper reading.'

'Did *he* see?'

'Yeah. Look, we'd better get her out before she breaks anything else.'

I hear him take several more footsteps into the room.

'Elle?' the man raises his voice to address me from the foot of the tunnel. 'Are you okay in there?'

'Yes,' I reply, surprised to find I have any strength left to respond. My body feels completely spent, like I've just run a double marathon. I'm surprisingly cold and chills run down my spine as I consider the man's whispered words. He thinks I'm somehow to blame for this?

I'd felt an electric shock when my hand slammed against the machine, but those static sparks happen to everybody once in a while. While it was more painful than the occasional static electric shock you might get, it was hardly the kind of thing that could affect a machine like this. Or was it?

The table beneath me begins to move and I'm slowly pulled from the machine. The room is bright after the darkness of the tunnel and I embrace the relief I feel to be out of the scanner.

'The power on the machine is down, so we'll have to stop there for today,' the doctor explains. His eyes are narrowed on me keenly and he appears to be analysing my reaction closely. He doesn't seem alarmed by what happened, merely annoyed or inconvenienced.

'What happened?' I ask.

'Must be a power outage,' he says, fumbling over his explanation. 'They happen here every so often.'

I try not to show surprise on my face as I listen to his obvious lie. 'Does that mean I can go back to the ward now?'

The nurse and the doctor look at each other, something unsaid passing between them, before he slowly nods. 'Yes, that should be fine.'

I sigh, relieved to be getting away from the MRI machine as quickly as possible. I don't know how to reconcile with the memories that rose to the surface and bombarded my mind whilst in the machine. I remember finding Sebastian. I know about being caught and held in here for months, but I also know Sebastian's mum died of the same mutations that are killing me. Some of the details of what happened are still blurry, but I finally know the truth about this place and the people who run it. No one here can be trusted, that much at least is clear.

As the nurse wheels me from the room, I glance up at the long window that takes up the better half of one wall. The man in the suit still stands there and as I move past the window he slowly steps out of the shadows.

I freeze as I take in the features of his face. It's the man from my dream last night. I'd only seen him for a moment, but I'm certain it's him. He's easily in his fifties and the skin on his face is weather beaten, which is at odds with his perfectly trimmed beard and slick dark blonde hair.

I try to stay calm, but it's difficult to do so when the man of my nightmares has materialised in front of me. Chills run down my spine and my breathing hitches in my throat. How could I dream about this man before I ever saw him? And why is he here watching me now?

A manic grin slowly forms on his lips and his cunning, blue eyes watch me hungrily. I drop my gaze from his, not liking the way he watches me. I wrap my hands tightly around the armrests of the chair and try to remain composed as I leave the room. I may have my memories back, but knowing that the man from my dreams is real is all I can focus on.

I look down at my hands, which still tightly grasp the armrests of the chair and I swear I catch the tiniest fiery spark jump from one of them, fizzling quickly out of existence in the air just above my hand.

I frown and slowly pull the offending hand from the armrest to look at it closer. It looks normal. I turn it over to look at the side. Yes, completely normal. I shake my head and place the hand back down, unable to reconcile with what I just observed.

Was the doctor right? Is it my fault the MRI stopped working? I felt different in there; like something was stirring within me I'd never felt before. Was that something enough to break a scanner though? I'm not so sure, but the doctor was and he wasn't surprised. Neither was the nurse. If they are right, then they knew this was inside of me all along.

The sound of footsteps draws my attention away from my hands and I look up to the far end of the corridor as an orderly walks around the corner and approaches us. I almost drop my gaze in disinterest, but as my sight falls on the man's face I stop. A small gasp escapes my lips and my heart hammers against my ribs, because I know him. It's Ryan.

CHAPTER TEN

Ryan's eyes meet mine for the briefest of seconds, before coolly moving on to stare at the nurse behind me. There was no acknowledgment in his gaze. Not even the slightest hint he knew me at all. Did he even recognise me?

My heart pounds in my ears and my thoughts jumble as I try to understand. Is he here to help? Does he work here? I'm thrown by his presence. The last time I saw him he was guarding the front of the talented dorms dressed in a recruiter's uniform. Is he a recruiter? What could he possibly be doing in the hospital?

He glances at one of the doors in front of us before shaking his head and looking to one on the other side of the corridor, his lips pursed as he considers them. The nurse slows my wheelchair as we approach him and clears her throat.

'Are you looking for something?' she asks Ryan, slowing my chair to a stop.

'Yeah, something to do,' he chuckles.

'You're new here,' she states, rather than asks.

'That obvious, huh?'

She nods. 'The new recruits usually are. There's a nurses station down the corridor then to the right, they'll be able to tell you what they need help with.'

Ryan pauses. 'Why don't I help you transport the patient you've got? I'm sure you've got a million other things on the go.'

Her shoulders slouch with relief. 'You wouldn't mind?'

'It would be no problem,' he responds, grinning. 'We'd be helping each other out. Where is she going?'

'Back to the children's ward.'

'Which is...'

'In the north quadrant. Take a right up ahead and follow that corridor until you reach a T-junction. Go left and the children's ward is the door at the end.' The words are barely out of her mouth and she is already walking off in the other direction. 'Thanks,' she calls, with a dismissive wave of her hand.

Ryan takes hold of my wheelchair and slowly starts to move towards the children's ward. As soon as the nurse has rounded the corner he stops the chair and crouches down beside me.

'Are you alright Elle?' he asks.

'What are you doing here?' I ask, at the same time.

He glances over his shoulder, before turning back and looking me in the eyes. 'I'm here to get you out.'

I tilt my head as I look at him. 'I don't understand. How did you even know I was here?'

'That doesn't matter right now. What matters is we need to get out before they get the inhibitor sensors back up and running, and my talent becomes useless.' He holds out his hand to me, but I hesitate.

'Is what's going on here that bad?' Everything inside me has been screaming this place is wrong, but I haven't found anything concrete to prove it. I think of the man from my dreams and shudder. Could Ryan get me away from here? Away from him?

'It's not good. These are bad people. Their experiments are making you sick. I'm here to get you out.'

'Experiments? I thought they were treatments to make me better?'

His words seem to click into place with everything I already know about the hospital.

'I haven't got time to explain. Just trust me, they don't care about your health,' he says, his eyes begging me to believe him. 'We need to go and this may be our only chance.'

'Okay,' I agree. 'But, we can't go without Will or Kelsey.'

He pulls back and stares me down. 'You want me to get your friends out?' he asks. 'Are you kidding me?

'I can't leave them here. Especially not after what you've just told me...'

He stands and swears, taking several steps away before swinging back to face me. 'We don't have time to get them, but I could come back for them, just let me take you now.'

I shake my head and cross my arms over my chest. 'If I escape with you now, security in here is bound to increase and getting them out may not be possible. I won't risk it. If you can't help the three of us I'll have to find another way.'

Ryan almost growls in response. His expression quickly changes though. He stands straighter and the anger on his face drops.

'They're turning the inhibitors back up. This is your last chance.' He holds out his hand to me, but I shake my head. 'Fine, midnight tonight I'll come for you in the children's ward. You just need to find a way to turn the inhibitor off in there.'

'But how do I do that?' I ask, my words meeting empty air as Ryan vanishes from before me. I blink and look over my shoulder, up and down the corridor, feeling a little stunned and suddenly very alone.

I take a deep breath and slowly blow it out. I need to figure out what he meant about the inhibitor sensors in the ward and I don't have much time to do it in.

'What are you doing out here alone?' a woman bellows. I turn and watch as a nurse rushes up to me. 'Well?' she emphasises, when I don't respond.

I shrug. 'The orderly who was returning me to the children's ward disappeared.' Literally.

The nurse tuts and mutters about how unreliable the orderlies in this place are. She bumps my cuff against her tablet, taking a look at it closely, 'I'll take you back now.'

WHEN WE ENTER the ward Kelsey, who is sitting on the end of Will's bed, jumps up and rushes over to me. 'Why were you gone for so long?' she asks, as the nurse pushes my chair down the aisle. She's been up and out of bed today, and looking a lot better than she was.

'I had to go for some tests and they took a little while,' I respond.

She frowns and casts her eyes down to the floor. She used to talk excitedly about going for tests because of the sweets she'd get, but she seems troubled by the idea now. It only makes me worry more about what happened to her when she was gone.

The nurse steadies my chair as I move across to my bed. Even just the small movement from one spot to the other is more exhausting than I'm happy to admit.

'How did it go?' Will asks, as I slide under the covers.

'It was fine,' I respond. The nurse continues to hover over me, reconnecting my IV drip. I glance at the liquid in the tube apprehensively, but don't make a move to stop her. I can't raise any suspicion now.

'What's been happening in here?' I ask, as the nurse moves away to answer a comm.

'Not much,' Will responds. 'Although I was lucky to have Kelsey here keeping me company.'

Kelsey's face lights up when she hears this and she stares at him adoringly. For a four-year-old she seems convinced she's going to marry Will when she grows up.

'Well, sounds like I left you in very capable hands,' I respond.

Kelsey nods eagerly, but her attention seems to be drifting from us to a group of girls who have just brought a board game out on one of their beds.

'You should go play with them Kels,' Will suggests. She doesn't need telling twice and quickly disappears to join them.

'Dr. Milton will be by to see you in about an hour,' the nurse says, as she disconnects her comm and walks back to take the wheelchair from my bedside.

My shoulders tense at her words. 'Why is he coming to see me?' I ask. I haven't seen him since I arrived and it's odd he'd choose now of all times to come for a chat. My heart beats faster. Has he been told what happened in the MRI scanner? Could he know some of my memories have returned?

'Just a check up,' she answers, turning away and moving towards the door before I can ask her anything else.

'Why *is* he coming to see you?' Will asks, once she's out of the room.

'I have no idea,' I answer, though it's not the complete truth. I suspect he wants to see me after what happened in the scanner or *worse*, if he knows Ryan contacted me, but I can't tell Will about it right now. Not when anyone could overhear.

He gives me a worried look. 'He never comes to visit kids in here,' he says.

'I'm sure it's nothing.'

He pauses, looking away from me. 'You've been getting really sick whenever you come back from a treatment,' he says. 'Could that be why?' He can barely look at me as he says it, like it's wrong to think it, let alone say the words aloud.

'Maybe,' I respond.

'I've been getting worse,' he says, his voice quieter than it was before. 'What they are doing to us doesn't seem to be making us much better.'

He glances at me, a look of total helplessness in his eyes. He looks

73

like he wants to give up all hope of recovering, like he doesn't believe there's any chance of him getting better.

'I know,' I respond, unable to bring myself to tell him just how right he is. My only consoling thought is their experiments on him will stop tonight.

CHAPTER ELEVEN

When Dr. Milton arrives I'm completely worked up about his visit. I feel convinced he's coming to interrogate me about what happened in the scanner. Will I be in trouble? Could he suspect I know more than I've let on? Maybe he is just coming to check on me?

'I hear there was a problem in the MRI today,' Dr. Milton says, as he approaches. He brings a chair over and places it down next to the bed. Taking a seat, he puts his tablet down on his lap and watches me.

'Yes, they said there was a power failure,' I respond, repeating the doctor's explanation. My heart beats quickly in my chest. It beats so hard and fast that I swear the doctor can hear my nerves in its unnatural beat.

'Were you okay in there?' he asks, the picture of concern.

'A little scared. I was glad when I got out. I really don't do well in confined spaces.'

He pauses. 'Nothing *strange* happened?' he asks.

I swallow and raise my gaze to meet his own. 'I wasn't feeling well because I was scared, and then the lights went out and the machine stopped. Apart from that, nothing strange happened.'

He eyes me closely, before sitting further back in his chair. 'Well, I'm sorry you suffered such a scare. We'll try to avoid the MRI machine now we know how it upsets you.'

I nod. 'I'd rather not go in there again.' I glance over the doctor's shoulder to look at Will, who sits watching us attentively from behind. His eyes are filled with questions, and I feel bad for not explaining to him what happened in the scanner earlier. But a part of me is grateful he doesn't need to be worried by the truth. He seems surprised by our conversation, but not concerned.

'We'll try our best,' Dr. Milton responds. 'Now, have you had any of your memories come back? I know you were concerned about forgetting a few things when we last met.'

My gaze jolts back to look at the doctor and I frown at his question. Does he know? 'No. Nothing.'

'Nothing today when you were scared? Sometimes fear can cause supressed memories to be recalled.' He seems calm and together as he asks me these things, but I notice his hands grip his tablet tightly and the skin across his knuckles is turning white. He's worried. He's not the only one.

'No. I haven't remembered anything,' I lie. 'Should I remember something by now?'

'Not necessarily,' he replies, his grip relaxing slightly and the skin across his knuckles turning from white back to pink. 'It's perfectly normal. These things can sometimes take a while. Hopefully they will come back soon.'

'Yeah, hopefully,' I agree. Although, I get the feeling that's the last thing he wants. Despite remembering how I came to be in the hospital, I feel like there is still something missing. The memories of my initial six weeks in the hospital are murky at best. What did they do to me during that time? Maybe I'm struggling to recall anything because I'm not sure if I want to remember?

'Well, I'm glad to see how well you're doing and I'm sorry about the scare you had today,' he says, standing and folding his arms over his chest. 'If you ever need anything, send one of the nurses for me.'

'I will,' I reply, knowing perfectly well *that* will not happen.

The doctor leaves and I try to calm my frayed nerves and relax. He didn't know about Ryan. At least that was one thing I didn't need to worry about.

'What happened Elle?' Will asks.

I look over to him as he stares aimlessly into space, a frown on his face. 'What do you mean?'

'It's pretty clear something happened to you in the MRI machine today. Dr. Milton doesn't come for a "check up" over nothing. What happened?'

I glance uneasily at the door the doctor just left through. 'I don't know for sure. My hand touched the wall and I got an electric shock from the machine. Then it powered down.' I shake my head. 'But that's the least of my worries right now.'

'Why?'

I glance around the room, before hopping off my bed to sit on Will's. 'Because my memories are back and we need to get out of here,' I whisper to him, keeping my voice low so the other kids won't hear.

'What do you mean?' he asks, his raised whisper drawing the attention of the boy half-snoozing in the bed on the other side of his. Luckily, the boy rolls over, completely disinterested in anything Will and I may be discussing.

Will gives me an apologetic look.

I lower my voice even further. 'This place isn't what it seems and we need to leave.'

'Why are you suddenly saying this?' he asks. I can see he's trying to stay calm, but from the way his words rush out it's clear he's failing to maintain his composure. Will has trusted these people for such a long time and it's obvious that telling him otherwise is upsetting him, but he needs to know the truth.

'Because I now know they lied about how I came to the hospital. I was in here for six weeks before I met you, but they somehow erased my memory of it. They aren't treating us because we're sick. They're experimenting on us, like lab rats. Someone I trust, confirmed it all to me today.'

I half expect Will's face to inappropriately light up at the mention of rats, but instead his eyes darken. 'Why would they lie?'

'I don't know,' I reply, wishing I had more answers for him. 'But I've had a bad feeling about the treatments we've been getting for a while now, and if Ryan tells me this place is bad, I believe him.'

'How does he know all this?'

'I'm not certain, he didn't have time to explain, but he wouldn't lie to me. He said they didn't care about our health at all, and judging by how no kids ever seem to walk out of this place, I have to agree.'

Will's shoulders slouch. 'Do you think the experiments are the reason I'm getting so sick?' His voice is fragile; it reminds me how young he is. How little he deserves what's happening to him.

'I think so,' I reply, at a loss for better words to respond with. I pull my knees up to my chest and hug them close, feeling physically and emotionally exhausted.

I stop myself from looking around the room at the other kids. I don't want to leave them here and none of them deserve this treatment, but I have no idea how I could possibly get them all out. If Ryan is teleporting us, he won't have time to rescue them all.

'How do we get out?' Will asks.

I sigh and try to push the guilt I feel for abandoning a room full of children to the back of my mind. 'Ryan broke in here using his talent, and he can break us out. He said we need to turn off the inhibitor sensor in here and he'll come get us at midnight. But I have no idea what it looks like or how to turn it off. Do you have any ideas?'

'No,' he says, frowning as he looks around the room. The place is so bland and empty, but for the kids and the beds. You'd think the inhibitor sensors would be obvious. 'Do you know what they look like?'

I purse my lips. 'I have no idea and I didn't have a chance to ask.'

'Do you think maybe that's them?' he asks, pointing to the two darkened glass cylinders that are fixed to the wall above the door. The glass is highly reflective and you can't see what's inside.

'I assumed they were cameras,' I reply.

'Don't you think if they had cameras in here watching us they would have come for Kelsey a whole lot sooner when she was sick.'

'Perhaps they weren't watching them?'

'Maybe,' he concedes. 'I don't know, I just have a feeling about them. They look slightly longer and thinner than the regular domes you'd find cameras in.'

'You think?' I ask, scratching my head. They seem pretty similar to me. 'But, how can we know for sure?'

'I guess we can't,' he replies.

I stand and walk over to the door to get a better look at the cylinders. There's nothing particularly special about them, they just look like glass covers. I squint my eyes to try and see through the reflective casing, but only see my face along the shiny surface.

I slowly walk back to Will, feeling defeated. 'I couldn't see anything, but it's our best shot. How do we turn them off?'

'I think I have an idea,' Will replies, with a smile.

CHAPTER TWELVE

I n the middle of the night, when I'm certain the other children are asleep, I creep over to Will's bed. As I approach his sleeping form I feel my resolve to escape strengthen. He's been getting increasingly worse this last week. He needs help. We both do.

Looking down at him I feel unsure of the most appropriate way to wake the sleeping boy up. He looks peaceful and I feel bad disturbing his much needed rest, but we only have a short time until midnight. We need to get moving.

'Will,' I whisper to him. 'Will! Wake up.'

He mumbles quietly in his sleep before continuing to softly snore.

I gently shake his arm. 'Will?'

He groans and rolls towards me. 'What do you want Elle?' he grumbles, rubbing his eyes tiredly.

'We need to get going.'

His eyes open, wide-awake and he nods seriously.

As I follow him to the door, I look around the room at all the other kids, guilt consuming me as I think about leaving them here.

This needs to stop, but there's nothing I can do to help them from inside this place.

I creep over to Kelsey's bed and slowly lift her sleeping body into my arms.

'What going on?' she asks, her words garbled in the massive yawn she's taking.

'We're going on a little trip,' I respond.

Her eyes light up. 'And Will's coming?' she checks.

'And Will's coming,' I confirm, much to her delight. Now she's more awake I lower her to the ground to stand next to me as I peer up at the glass cylinders above the door. They hadn't seemed so high up earlier today, but now we're closer they seem impossibly far.

'So, what's this big plan of yours? How do you think we turn them off?' I whisper to Will.

'All over it,' he murmurs, nodding his head at the metal IV stand in his hands.

'What do you plan to do with that?'

Will doesn't answer. Instead, he swings the large metal stand and hits the first cylinder case. He quickly follows up by swinging again to break the other.

The loud smashing sound wakes several of the other kids up. Some squeal with fear and others start crying. Kelsey hugs my leg tightly.

'Do you think that did it?' Will asks, placing the stand on the ground.

'I don't know,' I worry. There doesn't appear to be cameras inside either of the cylinders, but Ryan hasn't appeared either. 'What if they're not the inhibitors? What if we were wrong?' If they were cameras, someone must have seen us by now.

I try to take a calming breath, but I can feel blood pulsing quickly through my body and the ends of my fingers feel like they're throbbing.

'Wait,' Will says. 'I don't think one of the sensors broke on impact.' He grabs the metal stand and reaches up, throwing his body into the movement as he smashes the sensor with the stand.

A loud siren begins whooping. I throw my hands up over my ears and try to stop myself from yelling out in pain. It's so loud I think I will be sick.

'What now?' Will shouts to me, over the deafening noise.

'I don't know! He didn't tell me what comes next. He just said he'd be here.' A loud banging comes from the other side of the door followed by a shattering sound as the wood around the frame and handle cracks and the door opens to reveal Ryan standing there.

I rush towards him. 'You came,' I say, relieved this wasn't all for nothing.

'Of course I came,' he replies, surprised I ever doubted him.

There's a tug at my pants as we exit the room and I look down to see Kelsey there. 'Who's he?' she asks.

I quickly take her hand and give it a little squeeze. 'This is Ryan. He's the man who's going to help us get out of here,' I respond.

'How do we do this?' I ask, turning to face Ryan.

'We'll teleport,' he says. 'I can only do it one at a time though, and we need to do it before the inhibitor sensors are up again or someone comes. Elle?' he turns and holds his hand out to me.

'No, take Will first.'

'There isn't time to argue about this, take my hand Elle!'

'You should go Elle,' Will agrees.

I step back from Ryan and push Will forward. 'Just take Will. He's been the sickest. I'll see you when you get back.'

Ryan growls and grabs Will's hands. 'I need you to close your eyes and hold my hand tight. Okay?'

Will nods and shuts his eyes. Ryan fixes his gaze on me. 'If someone comes or if I'm not back in two minutes, get back in the room. We'll find another way.'

Moments later the two of them disappear from sight. Kelsey squeals, causing me to jump.

'What's wrong?'

'Where did they go?' she asks.

'Ryan has taken Will to a place away from the hospital where he will be safe. He'll be right back and then it will be your turn. Do you think you can be brave and go with Ryan for me?'

'Uh-huh,' she agrees.

After a minute of waiting, Kelsey tugs my arm. 'When is he coming back?' she asks.

'I don't know,' I respond, looking up and down the corridor. He should be back by now. I try not to worry about what could be keeping him, but it's hard to avoid. What will we do if he doesn't come back for us?

I turn to look at the ward, but pause as I catch the sound of something in the distance, slowly getting louder. I tilt my ear in the direction of the noise and focus in on the constant slapping sound I can just make out over the sound of the alarm. As it continues to grow louder and clearer I realise what it is—footsteps. Lots of them.

I instinctively grip Kelsey's hand tighter. There are people coming this way and we can't be out here when they arrive.

I consider the children's ward for a brief moment, before looking to the corridor beyond. My heart thunders in my chest as I look to the empty passage that leads away from the ward and the people heading in our direction.

Ryan said to go back in the room and we'd find another way. But, as I look at Kelsey, I know I can't let her spend another day in this place. We need to find a way out now, with Ryan's help or not.

Kelsey's lower lip trembles. 'Where's Ryan?'

'No idea, but we don't have time to wait and find out. We have to go!' I pull her hand and start running in the opposite direction, heading away from the people coming towards the children's ward.

Kelsey is so little, and running so slowly, I grab her up in my arms to carry her. Her weight is no problem and she barely slows me down as the adrenaline pulses through me, pushing me to run faster.

I turn the corner, glancing back just in time to see several men in uniform appear at the other end of the children's ward corridor. I don't think they've seen me, but I can't take any risks so I continue to run, fear for Kelsey driving me to move faster.

The sound of shouting from the children's ward reaches my ears as the men arrive to investigate the alarm, but I don't turn around. I can't go back, even though I wish I could. I try to shut out the screams of fear from the children as a mob of men rush into the room. They don't deserve this and my heart breaks. I can't fix it.

Kelsey and I reach a junction and I race forward without giving any thought of which route to go, but Kelsey shakes my arm.

'We shouldn't go this way,' she says.

'Why not?' I ask, stopping.

She shrugs. 'We just shouldn't. I get a bad feeling.'

Her face is serious and as I look in her eyes I get a strong feeling in my gut that I should believe her. I nod and start running down the other corridor.

The place is a dead end. I race to the closest door to try the door handle, but it's locked. Then I move onto the next, finding it locked as well.

I curse. I have no idea how to get out of this place. What happened to Ryan? Why didn't he make it back for us?

'We need to go in there,' Kelsey says, as we move past one of the doors. I try the handle, but it's locked. Fear pulses through me. Are we cornered here? Is there no way out?

My breathing shortens and I rattle the handle violently, trying to get it to open. My fingertips tingle from the movement and static energy prickles along my arms as I concentrate on the handle. The more I rattle it, the greater frustration I feel for the small object baring our way. I put Kelsey down and, still gripping the door handle, I ram my shoulder into the heavy wooden door.

'Please, just open!' I yell at the door, my anger seeming to pulse like thick and violent energy that radiates out of my skin.

I jump back in shock as a light bulb flickers and then explodes with a loud crack behind me, plunging the section of corridor into darkness. At the same time, the keypad by the door sparks and bursts into flames.

'Cool,' Kelsey whispers.

I stare at the mangled mess of a security pad and take an unconscious step further away from it. I didn't think I could feel any more fear in this moment, but I was mistaken. The anger I felt mere seconds ago has evaporated and been replaced by cold terror. Did I do that? I remember what happened in the MRI machine and my hands shake as I pull Kelsey close to me.

'We should go inside,' she says. Apparently not even slightly concerned I just managed to turn a security pad into liquid.

I nod, feeling almost robotic as I move forwards and twist the door handle. The door opens onto a messy lab, with benches covered in large machines, piles of loose papers and beakers of all shapes and sizes. A man dressed in a white lab coat weaves his way between the benches towards us, clearly wanting to see what the commotion is.

He stops as we enter and his eyes latch onto mine. 'Who are you?' he asks. 'You can't be in here.'

I fail to answer him though, because I've seen his face before. It's been such a long time since I looked at the picture Dr. Wilson gave me in the ARC, should I ever find his grandson, but there's no mistaking the resemblance to the man I see before me.

'You're not allowed to be out of your ward. We need to get you back there at once.'

'Aiden?' I say.

The colour in his face drains and his eyes fill with fear. 'How do you know my name?'

CHAPTER THIRTEEN

iden rushes towards me and grabs my free arm, pulling me further into the room. 'How do you know my name?' he repeats.

'It's really you!' I exclaim, unable to believe I've found him. He's in his early twenties and a few years older than in the picture I'd been given. There's a hardness in his eyes the picture didn't portray and he seems incredibly serious, but it's really him.

'You look so much like your grandfather,' I say.

'You know him?' he asks, the grip on my arm loosening.

'Yes, in the ARC. I met him in the Aged Care Ward.'

He frowns. 'I'm calling the nurses. You need to get back to your room.'

'Wait!' I yell, holding out my hand to stop him. I glance back over my shoulder to the door. 'Please don't, let me explain. I have something you'll want to hear.'

'I highly doubt that,' he responds, lifting his cuff to look at the screen.

'Your grandfather wanted me to give you a message.'

'What are you talking about?' he asks, glancing up at me from his cuff.

'Your grandfather, Dr. Wilson, helped me escape the ARC. He gave me a picture of you and drew a message for you on the back of it.

'What was the message?'

'I don't have it here, but I could draw it...' I hesitate. 'If you can you help us get out of here.'

Aiden looks around the room. 'That will be difficult,' he responds.

'Please. We can't stay here any longer, we need to get out.'

Aiden folds his arms across his chest. 'This isn't a game. That message could be important.'

'I know this isn't a game. I've been locked in this place against my will and experimented on for weeks now. I am more than aware how little this is a game. We've escaped and there are recruiters coming for us. You have to help us now or I won't be able to give you the message.'

His eyes soften as he looks at me. 'It's not simple. There's only one way out of here.'

'What is it?'

'It takes time, which you don't have. Recruiters will come and secure the rest of this floor, searching for you two. You maybe have a few minutes before you're found and I expect you'll be put in solitary for attempting to escape,' he says, nodding his head at me.

I ignore the way my heart falters as I consider time in solitary. 'How much time do you need?'

'It's not *me* that needs it. The only way out is from the outside.'

'I don't understand.'

'This place is completely walled in. The only way out is with someone talented who can get in and out either by teleporting or walking through the walls. There is one spot this can happen at, that doesn't constantly have the inhibitor sensors on, and it's heavily guarded.'

'So, it's possible,' I conclude.

'Yes. It's possible.'

'How long will it take?'

He scratches his face. 'I don't know, maybe a few hours. I have contacts on the outside, but it depends on them.'

I hear footsteps from far down the hallway. 'People are coming this way. What do we do?'

His eyes flick up to look at the door behind me. 'The only way out is back the way you came, if they're already here there's no escape.'

I glance over my shoulder to the door. 'Then we're doomed.'

Kelsey lets out a little whimper and I lift her up in to my arms. 'It will be okay.'

The men outside the room shout to each other as they discover the broken security pad at the entrance to the lab.

I face them as they burst into the room. There are six of them by the door, all dressed in black, their faces filled with outrage.

'What are you doing in here?' the man in front yells.

'Elle?' Kelsey whispers to me, her small voice shaking, as they move closer.

'It's going to be fine,' I respond, gripping her more tightly in my arms. I look up to the men moving towards us. 'I'm sorry we're out of our room. We were scared when the siren went off. We thought there might be a fire and got lost trying to get away.'

'She's right, I was just about to bring the girls back to their room...' Aiden says.

'Give the girl to us,' one of the men says to me, ignoring Aiden.

I take a step backwards. 'No, I won't leave her with you.'

One of the men disappears and reappears next to me. Before I can react, he wrenches Kelsey from my arms, disappears again and reappears behind the others.

Kelsey screams and starts to cry.

'Please don't hurt her!' I shout out. As I do the light bulb above my head explodes and glass shatters over my head. I throw my arms over my face to cover it from the shards that fly down on me.

'Will someone get an inhibitor out!'

I drop my arms from around my head and look up at one of the recruiters who is taking hesitant steps towards me. He holds his arms out in front of him and a black glass contraption glints in his hands.

'I need you to calm down. Nothing bad will happen to you or your friend, we're just taking her back to the children's ward. We want to make sure she's okay.'

My hands feel like they are pulsing with anger and energy. I instinctively hold them out in front of me in defence as the recruiter takes a step nearer. 'Don't come any closer!' I warn.

'We know you were trying to escape,' the man says. 'But, everything will be okay if you just calm down and come with us.'

'No!' I roar. A tremor ripples through the room, as though it has been shaken by the very sound of my voice, causing me to stumble backwards against one of the benches. A slow rumbling noise echoes as the room continues to quake and small cracks splinter out on the ground around my feet. Several beakers roll off the table, their glass shattering in a high-pitched clamour when they hit the ground.

My mind feels foggy and I struggle to think clearly. I notice the man take another step nearer. 'I said, don't come any closer!'

A hissing noise reaches my ears and I glance down at my hands. Where I have placed them on the metal bench looks like it has been covered in a layer of shimmering blue frost that slowly expands outwards, reaching for the broken shards of glass that lie just beyond. I rip my hands away, looking at the two things with fear.

'I said, don't...' I stagger forwards and sway on my feet. My head fills with a shooting pain and I drop to my knees, clawing my hands against my forehead, willing it to stop.

'Make it stop, please make it stop,' I beg.

My body starts convulsing and I sink onto the floor. My world is filled with pain, my skin blazing with heat and searing with cold all at once. I scream as my body buckles and all the pent up energy swelling inside me escapes in one powerful surge. I feel it scorching me as it rips through my skin, leaving the air around me cold. I collapse back against the ground, feeling completely empty inside.

As I succumb to the welcome invitation of the darkness that pulls me under I feel something cool slipped onto my wrist and the buzzing feeling disappears as I black out.

CHAPTER FOURTEEN

'Why is she still sleeping?' I hear Kelsey ask, her high-pitched voice dips and rises in the singsong way it does, so I immediately recognise it.

'I think she's waking up now,' comes a man's response.

I slowly blink my eyes open to see Aiden and Kelsey looking down at me from above. The room is dark and a soft blue light illuminates their faces. While Kelsey beams at me, Aiden's forehead is furrowed with a frown. 'You're Elle Winters, aren't you?' he asks.

I slowly nod. 'What happened?' I croak.

'You exploded,' Kelsey says, her eyes twinkling with excitement.

'I what?' I shift my attention from Kelsey to Aiden.

'You used one of your talents and it didn't end well. We need to get you out of here,' Aiden explains.

'Talents? What did I do?' I ask, sitting up so quickly blood rushes to my head. 'Woah,' I whisper, as I get a look at the room around me. Though the room is darkened, blue emergency lights glow down upon a sparkling white blanket of snow and ice that appears to cover everything. Like one of the impact winter storms had erupted inside the room, the place looks like it's been hit by a blizzard.

My eyes drop onto a frozen statue before me. I can just make out the features of one of the recruiters who'd been closest to me before I passed out. 'I did that to him?' I ask, tears creeping into the corners of my eyes as I start shaking. 'Is he going to be okay?'

'They'll get a crew in here,' Aiden says, gently putting his hand on my shoulder. 'I'm sure they'll be able to help him and the others.'

'You should've seen yourself!' Kelsey exclaims. 'It was *awesome!*'

My attention moves to Kelsey and I grab her arms to inspect her for any damage I inflicted. 'How aren't you hurt?' I ask. 'You were just there!'

'You would never hurt me,' she says simply.

'This is incredible,' Aiden's voice interrupts. 'I've heard about you from the other doctors. You're the one they talk about.'

'What do you mean?'

'Your mutation is different to the others here. You're special. They have been trying to give you talents, and it has obviously worked. I doubt you'll ever see the outside of a lab again if they see this. Who knows what else you can do.'

'But... why me?'

'Your mutation allows you to absorb and adapt to other talents.' His eyes light up as he says this. 'They've been talking about you for weeks. You're vital to their research and if they see how well it's working they'll step up their experiments. Like I said, you need to leave.'

I try to understand what he's just said, but right now it feels beyond me. His words feel as though they are spoken in a foreign language. He may think I'm special, talented even, but I feel like I'm a monster.

'I've already contacted someone on the outside who can help. It's not ideal, and it's risky, but we'll have to make do with what we've got. If they catch you now, there will be no escape.'

I nod, trying to gather my frayed nerves together and compose myself. I slowly draw myself up and stand, though I feel unsteady on my feet. 'What do we do?'

'Follow me,' he replies, making his way past the frozen bodies to the door that leads back to the corridor.

The passage is pitch black and silent; the siren that sounded earlier now gone. Kelsey shuffles closer, gripping my hand tightly in hers as Aiden lights up his cuff and flashes the beam into the darkness. I look down to do the same with my own, but my cuff is gone and on my wrist is a contraption I haven't seen before.

'What's this?' I ask, lifting my wrist closer to inspect it. It's similar to my usual cuff, but thinner and instead of clear glass it's black. It looks like the device that had been in the recruiter's hand before.

Aiden turns back, flashing the light onto the device.

'It's a wearable inhibitor, it will stop your talents so we don't have a repeat of what happened in my lab.'

'Did you put this on me?'

'Yes. It's for your own safety,' he replies. 'Come on, we have to move quickly now.'

We make our way through the darkened building slowly, constantly checking for other doctors and recruiters. The hallways are deserted though and the emptiness sets me on edge.

'Why is it so dark?' Kelsey asks.

'I think you can thank Elle's little performance back there for the darkness,' Aiden replies. 'Though I'm surprised the generators haven't kicked in out here.'

I don't know if it's the eerie silence, the darkness or the fact I caused the building to completely black out, but shivers creep down my spine. I shouldn't be able to cause this. No one should.

'Where is everyone?' I ask, keeping my voice quiet. We haven't heard so much as a whisper since leaving Aiden's lab and it's making me nervous.

'I don't know,' he replies, his unease obvious.

'Surely they would have come running after I "exploded" as Kelsey put it.'

He glances back at me, before turning and moving forward. 'I have no clue where they all are.'

I become increasingly nervous. This has all gone *way* too smoothly so far. We're almost to the end of a corridor when the light from another cuff appears around the corner revealing a doctor coming towards us. The three of us freeze, becoming statues as the man approaches.

'Follow my lead,' Aiden whispers. 'And keep your head down, we can't have him seeing who you are.'

'Is that you Aiden?' the doctor says, as he gets close.

'Yeah,' Aiden responds.

I hold my breath as we continue towards the man.

'Absolute nightmare this is, isn't it?' he says, raising his hand to indicate the darkness.

'Definitely,' Aiden responds.

The man lifts his light to shine down on the faces of Kelsey and me. I keep my eyes glued to the floor. 'Who are they?'

'Just two patients. I'm returning them to their room.'

The man takes a step closer, the beam of light upon my face becoming brighter.

'I thought we had nurses for that,' he says.

Aiden smiles pleasantly. 'Well, nurses are a little hard to come by in the dark.'

The light drops from my face. 'I suppose so. Well, don't take too long returning them, the staff have all been told to stay in their rooms. Don't want to be caught out here when the squad arrives.' The man sounds nervous and he glances anxiously around as though expecting someone to jump out at him from the shadows.

Aiden's back stiffens. 'No, I suppose not. I'll see you later.'

'Okay,' the man replies, as he continues on his way.

'That was close,' I say, once we're clear of him.

'We need to hurry,' Aiden says. 'If the squad are on their way we don't have much time.'

'Who are the squad?' I ask, walking quickly to keep up with Aiden.

'They're the guys you send when all hell breaks loose.'

'That doesn't sound promising.'

'It's not.'

We move through the hospital as quickly as we dare in the dark. Aiden slows when he sees a lit corridor up ahead. He nods in its direction. 'You turn right at the end of the corridor and the bridge is the first door on the left.'

'What bridge?'

He goes to respond, but pauses and then glances over his shoulder, peering into the darkness behind us. His eyes search the shadows as though expecting to find someone there, and my heartbeat quickens as I turn and follow his gaze.

I don't see any movement or hear any sound other than the soft, almost inaudible breaths of Aiden and Kelsey beside me. Aiden taps my shoulder and jerks his head at the door closest to us. 'I don't think there's anyone around, but we'll go in here just to be safe,' he whispers.

I nod and, holding Kelsey's hand tight, follow him into what appears to be another lab. Aiden shines the light from his cuff around the room, before allowing us inside. He's quick to find the emergency lights in the lab and turns them on, illuminating the space in a soft blue light.

'You were going to tell us about the bridge?' I prompt him.

'Yes, it's the entry and exit room for the facility. It's your only way out and you need to get in there to meet my contact who's coming to get you. Once you're out of here, you should stay with them. We don't fully understand the consequences of the experiments yet. You need help that only they can give.'

He moves back to the door, but I reach out and grab his arm. 'Wait, are you leaving us?'

His eyes soften. 'I need to create a distraction as the bridge will be guarded, but I'll be back.' He glances at his cuff. 'The contact is meeting you at 1:00 A.M., which is in twenty minutes time, but we should aim to leave here ten minutes before that. If I'm not back...'

'You'll be back,' I say, my words sounding more certain than I feel. Anything could happen in the next twenty minutes.

'If I'm not...'

'Here,' I rush over to one of the desks in the room and grab a piece of paper to draw his grandfather's message on. I easily recall the strange design, a thick vertical black line with a triangle hanging from the top. I have no idea what it could mean, but it must mean something to Aiden. Once I've drawn it, I carefully fold the piece of paper and turn to hold it out to him. 'You should have this.'

He looks at the piece of paper in my hands eagerly, then shakes his head. 'No, I'll be back in time.'

'Aiden, you should take it.' I try to put it in his hands, but he refuses to accept it.

'No, not until you're safely in the hands of the people who are getting you out of here.'

'Okay,' I say, putting it in my pocket. 'You should go. We haven't got long.'

'It should only take me ten minutes, but if I'm not back—'

'We'll go,' I say, finishing his sentence. 'You'll be back. We'll see you soon.'

At least, I hope we will.

CHAPTER FIFTEEN

A iden disappears out the door and I place Kelsey up on one of the benches, jumping up to sit on it next to her. The lab seems similar to Aiden's. Then again, all labs in this place look the same to me.

It's unnerving being in such a large and darkened space so late at night with no one else around. I keep an ear out for Aiden's return, but so far there's been nothing.

As I wait, I continually eye the inhibitor band Aiden put on my wrist. What happened earlier was completely out of my control. I had no idea what was inside of me—I guess I still don't know what is. If what Aiden said is anything to go by, whatever they've put inside me is completely unnatural and too much for me to handle.

I run my fingers along the black band. It's strange how one small item could make such a large change in me. I shake my head. It is way less strange than a talent that can create a blizzard.

I check the time on the clock that hangs on the wall. Aiden still has time to get back here, before we need to leave. I can't imagine what kind of distraction he's thinking of. Half the facility is blacked out and all of the staff have been told to stay in their rooms. What more of a distraction would you need than that?

I try not to worry about what he's got planned or the possibility the recruiters won't leave their post by the bridge, but it's kind of hard not to. So many things could happen now and the chances of us getting out seem slim to none at all.

I look down at Kelsey who has fallen asleep, her body is curled up and her head rests on my lap. For her sake, I hope we get out of here. If they did something to her, because of me, I'd never forgive myself.

Another five minutes passes with no change. 'What is he doing?' I mutter, under my breath.

What if the person coming to rescue us arrives and we're not there? Will they leave without us? What if the squad arrives and finds us before we have a chance to escape?

I need to stop freaking out now, but looking at the time only makes me worry even more. Tonight has already been such a disaster, but it could still get worse from here.

Would removing the inhibitor band help? Would it protect us if I were able to use whatever talent I have inside? What if it's our only way out?

I lift my hand to slowly take it off my wrist.

'You shouldn't do that,' Kelsey says, stifling a yawn.

'You don't think?' I ask her.

She shakes her head and I place my hand back down by my side. She's probably right. It would only end badly. I look at the clock again. What is Aiden doing?

I stand and creep over to the door, opening it just a crack to have a look into the hallway. It's just as silent and dark out there as when we came through it.

A loud siren blares and I quickly close the door. He's done it. Well, he's done something. I check the time. He only has minutes to get back here though.

'We will be leaving in a minute,' I tell Kelsey, lifting her down from the table and getting her to follow me back to the door.

I try to listen for movement outside the room, but it's useless with the siren whooping loudly in the hallway. For a moment, I consider the band on my wrist again, but quickly dismiss any thoughts of taking it off. Removing the band is a last resort.

Glancing over my shoulder at the clock on the wall behind me, I check the time again. We have ten minutes until we need to meet Aiden's contact. We can't wait for him any longer. We have to leave now if we want to make it to the bridge in time.

I grasp the door handle and open the door, taking a cautious step as I lean out into the corridor and check for Aiden. There's no sign of him and my shoulders slouch with disappointment. We'll have to do this alone.

I take Kelsey's hand and lead her from the lab. We hurry to the junction at the end of the corridor, Kelsey having to run beside me to keep up with my quick pace. My heart beats unsteadily as I check over my shoulder into the empty passage behind us. There's still no sign of Aiden there.

When we reach the end of the corridor I pause before the junction. I'm about to peer out when Kelsey tugs my arm. I look down to find her shaking her head at me.

'We don't have any other choice,' I whisper. I glance around the corner and the corridor is empty. I pull back and pause before quickly checking again. Yes, there's no one there.

My fingers toy with the band on my wrist and I chew on my lower lip as I consider the device. I was only out of control when I'd been threatened earlier, maybe it will be useful to have it off just in case?

Before I can talk myself out of it, I take the band from my wrist and put it in my pocket.

The feeling of my talent being freed comes immediately. My blood feels electric in my body, surging powerfully through me and my hands feel like they are sparking with unbridled energy. I feel powerful yet overpowered all at once. It's brilliant and completely terrifying.

'Follow me, but not too closely,' I tell Kelsey, fearing if she comes too close I might hurt her.

I take cautious steps around the corner and my eyes latch onto the door before us. It's tantalisingly near and my heartbeat becomes quicker with each step closer we take. Energy ripples in the air around my fingers and I feel like I could almost reach out and grasp it if I tried.

I glance over at Kelsey who follows several steps behind me. She seems afraid and I wish I could hold her hand through this, but it feels too risky. Her eyes widen at something over my shoulder and a small gasp issues from her mouth. I whip my head around just as a recruiter grabs hold of my wrist.

'Are you the one they've been searching for?' He lifts his cuff to his mouth to talk into it, but my body reacts instinctively. The static energy I feel pulsing through my blood races through me towards the man's hand as it tightly grips my wrist.

It sizzles through the contact between us and I can feel the energy violently rippling across our connection. I don't know how to control it. I don't know how to stop it. I try to shake him off of me, but his grip on my wrist tightens as a thick layer of frost slowly covers his fingertips and works its way up his arm. His skin turns blue as icicles form on the hairs that cover his skin.

I jerk my wrist away from him, but it only seems to make it worse. Tiny sparks of electricity jump along the contact between us and they only grow larger in size, the longer he holds on.

The man screams and releases me. He drops to the floor writhing, as his body becomes half encased in ice and alight with electricity that dances across his skin like a storm of tiny thunderbolts. Eventually, he stops moving and I stagger backwards from him in shock.

I look up as Aiden races around the corner and pulls to a stop. 'I-I didn't mean to do that,' I stammer, looking back down at the man. 'I w-was scared and it just happened. I couldn't control it.'

'Get your inhibitor back on,' Aiden says, rushing to the man's side.

My hands shake as they fumble to grab the inhibitor out of my pocket and put it back on my wrist. I am calmer once it's back on, knowing my wild talents are contained again, but I still feel consumed by self-loathing at what I've done.

Aiden crouches beside the recruiter, placing two fingers against his neck. 'He's still alive. Barely, but he's still alive.' He stands and walks over to me. 'Elle, you can't blame yourself. It was an accident.'

'Was it?' I whisper. 'I knew taking that band off could end in someone getting hurt and yet I did it.'

'Here.' Aiden passes me a handkerchief and nods at my face. I frown and touch my nose. When I look at my fingers, the tips are covered in blood.

'Thanks,' I say, taking the handkerchief from him and pressing it against my nose.

'Is he sleeping?' Kelsey asks, in a small voice.

My stomach plummets as I look behind me. I'd forgotten she was there and the thought of her seeing what I've done makes me feel an intense wave of remorse.

Aiden saves me from answering. 'For a little while,' he says. He looks at his cuff, then to me. 'There are only a few more minutes until they arrive.'

We approach the door to the bridge, and Aiden places his cuff against the sensor by the door. I wait for the small beeping noise that the cuff has been accepted to sound, but nothing happens.

'What do we do?' I ask Aiden.

He looks as baffled as I am. 'I don't know,' he replies. 'My CommuCuff should work.' He places his cuff against the sensor again and once more it is rejected.

'The man has to open it,' Kelsey says.

We both look at her. 'What man?'

'The man on the other side.'

Aiden frowns at me.

'How do you know that?' I ask.

An element of doubt crosses her face and she looks down at her bare feet. 'Just a feeling.'

I crouch down so I'm eye level with her. 'Do you know when he will open it?'

She shakes her head.

Aiden bangs his fist against the door, but no one answers.

'Will you come with us?' I ask him.

'No, my people need someone inside the hospital, but I'll see you safely out of here first.'

'Your people?' I shake my head, dismissing the question. 'Aiden you should go before you get caught with us. We'll be fine waiting here until the door is open.'

He looks torn when he turns to face me. 'I want to make sure you get out of here.' He bangs his fist on the door again. 'Hello?' he shouts.

'You've done more than enough. Please go before you get in trouble. Here,' I stand and pass him the message from his grandfather that was tucked up in my pocket. 'I hope this was worth it.'

He grabs the paper eagerly, but doesn't open it. 'I didn't need this for it to be worth it. If I'd known who you were when you first barged into my lab, I would've helped without question. You deserve better than this Elle, you both do.' He pauses, looking at me closely, like he's imagining all the things they have done to me.

I fidget under the intensity of his gaze and look down at the paper, still folded in his hands. 'Are you going to open it?' I ask.

He smiles and nods, carefully opening the paper to look at the symbol drawn on the page. He frowns though and a look of utter confusion crosses his face.

'Are you sure this is the message?' he asks.

'Yes. I have no idea what it means though.'

He shakes his head. 'Neither do I ... unless ...'

'Unless what?' I ask, when he doesn't say anything more.

He studies the page closely, and then turns it around the other way as his eyes light up. 'He did it!'

'Did what?'

He brings the page over to me to show me the meaningless symbol I've drawn. 'It's an ancient rune,' he says, looking at me like the explanation for this is obvious. 'I should've recognised it as soon as I saw it. Grandad spent my entire childhood telling me stories and teaching me different runes. I was obsessed with them, but haven't looked at one in years.'

'But what does it mean?' I ask.

'This bit here,' he points to the long stick I've drawn, 'it means a wound. But, when joined with this bit here,' he points to the triangle, 'it means healing.'

'So...'

'When the two are combined together it means cure, which means my grandfather must have found it. It has to.'

'What cure?'

'What the doctors in here *should* be looking for: a way to stop the mutations altogether. If this is the cure, people in the ARC could return to the surface.' The excitement on his face drops and his skin pales. 'My grandfather's found the cure...'

'What's wrong?'

'I need to come with you, but there's someone I need to get!'

'What? Who?'

'I don't have time to explain,' he groans. 'But if there's any chance of a cure outside the walls of this hospital, she needs to leave tonight.' He starts running away from us, back towards the darkened corridor we'd just come down. 'Tell them to wait!'

As soon as he's around the corner though, the doorhandle rattles and the door to the bridge opens.

CHAPTER SIXTEEN

'Are you Elle?' the man standing in the doorway booms. His voice is strong and deep, and that only makes his giant frame even more intimidating. The guy is *huge*. He has an array of fearsome tattoos that cover his dark skin and he wears the kind of expression that would make the sturdiest recruiter re-evaluate their choice if pitted against him.

I nod, at a loss for words.

'This way,' he says. He stands back to reveal the bridge, which looks nothing like an actual bridge, but rather a small, empty room. Well, nearly empty.

'Beth?' I ask, as I enter the room and move past the man with Kelsey.

Beth runs towards me and throws her arms around my neck. 'I've been so worried!' she exclaims.

I immediately pull back and look at her closely. Did she hit her head? There's no way she would normally be this happy to see me. What is she even doing here? How did she get involved in this?

'You're Aiden's contact?' I ask her. 'How did you get here?'

'There'll be time for explanations later,' she says. 'We have to go.'

I glance back at the open doorway we've just come through. 'No, we can't go yet. Aiden told us to wait, he has to get someone and he'll be back any minute now.'

Beth barely bats an eyelid to consider what I've said. 'We can't wait. They've sent the squad and there aren't enough of us to fight them. Dalton,' she nods her head at the massive man who stands behind me, 'needs to open a window and we have to go.'

I stammer as I try to think of a way to stall Beth so Aiden has time to return, but she continues. 'The guy on the other side can't hold the bridge room for much longer. Let's go,' she commands Dalton.

Dalton walks up to the back wall and reaches his finger out to touch it. The tip of his forefinger glows blue and as he guides it up the wall a glowing trail appears in its wake. He continues slowly tracing until he's created a shimmering outline the size of a large door, which looks like it's been drawn on the wall with some kind of iridescent paint.

He places his other hand on the inside of the outline. Once it's pressed firmly against the wall it glows a bright and unearthly hue of blue and everything behind it dissolves like tiny grains of sand running through his fingers until there's nothing left at all.

A white room, almost identical to this one, is revealed on the other side. There's almost a shimmer to the air between the rooms and I can vaguely see the texture of the solid wall that was there before.

'Okay, you can go through,' Dalton says.

I look over my shoulder to the open doorway behind me and try to see if Aiden is on his way, but the doorway remains empty and there's no sign of him. He won't make it.

'Elle!' Beth grabs my arm, but I quickly yank it out of her grasp. 'We have to leave,' she urges.

My gaze darts to the doorway one last time. As I focus on the empty space, the alarm out in the hallway stops and an unnerving silence follows.

'We can't wait for him any longer. We have to go,' Beth says, her voice quieter and more urgent than before.

'I can't just leave him here,' I say. 'What if they find out he helped me escape?'

'If we don't leave now, none of us will be getting out. There's no way to know how far off he is or if he hasn't already been caught. Stop wasting time. People will get hurt the longer you stall. Don't make me use my talent on you,' she threatens.

'I thought you were an untalent?'

Beth raises an eyebrow at me.

'Right, obviously not,' I reply. 'Please, isn't there something we can do?'

Beth sighs. 'Look, as soon as you're out safely I'll see if we can send someone back for him, but right now we have to go.'

I watch her closely, and she seems sincere about sending someone for Aiden. 'Okay. We'll come.'

I walk towards Dalton, my hand gripped tightly around Kelsey's. Each step I take makes me feel increasingly guilty. I don't want to leave Aiden behind after he helped me, but Beth is right. He may already be caught. There's no way to know.

As we move through the window Dalton has created, a shiver passes through me and my body tingles. Once we're through, the feeling completely passes.

I watch Beth follow us through, and Dalton who comes behind her. I desperately hope Aiden will make it in time. But, the moment Dalton is no longer touching the empty space his hand stops glowing and the wall slowly reappears, speck, by tiny speck, until there's no opening at all.

'He can't leave it open?' I ask Beth.

She sadly shakes her head. 'No, his talent doesn't work that way I'm afraid.' She rubs my shoulder. 'Don't stress about him. Aiden has survived working in that place for a long time. He will be fine until we can send someone to get him out.'

'You don't know what it's like in there. If he's been caught chances are he won't.'

She looks away and focuses behind me on the wall we just came through. 'I know more about that place than anyone should.'

She doesn't let me question what she's said and immediately continues talking. 'This way,' she says, moving to the door at the other end of the room. 'Prepare yourself. It's not pretty out there. Make sure you keep close to me. If we come across trouble I'm your best chance of protection.'

I pick Kelsey up in my arms, uncertain what exactly it is we're preparing for. When Beth opens the door though, it's clear.

The hallway is lined with bodies on the ground. They are all clothed in the black recruiter's uniform, the same as those I'd seen in the hospital.

A man stands just outside the bridge room doorway. He's short with skin so pale it's almost blue and eyes as black as midnight. As soon as he sees us he raises his CommuCuff to his lips and talks quietly into it.

'That's Soren,' Beth says, nodding at him. He looks over at the sound of his name and catches me watching. I quickly look away.

I pull Kelsey close to me, hoping she doesn't see all the men lying stilly on the ground. As much as I want to, I doubt I can protect her from all of this. There are just too many of them.

'Are they dead?' I ask Beth.

'No, but I'm sure they wish they were.' She glances at the man talking into his cuff.

'What's his talent?' I whisper.

'You don't want to know,' she replies.

I shudder and make a mental note not to go anywhere near the guy. Beth starts moving down the corridor and I follow her closely, being careful not to step on any of the sleeping men. 'Will they wake up?' I ask.

'Eventually. None of them will be the same though.' She grimaces before turning to lead us down another corridor, which is thankfully free of bodies. Even Beth's steely exterior is shaken by what Soren can do. She's not the only one; the sight sent shivers down my spine and I even caught Dalton's face whiten when he got a look at all the men Soren had affected.

'Is there anyone else coming to help?' I ask Beth.

'No, it's just us, but we'll be fine.'

I want to ask if the people she's with are somehow connected with Ryan, but I'm not sure whether Dalton and Soren can be trusted. I'll have to wait until we're alone.

We quietly move through the hospital. There seems to be little difference to the hospital on this side of the bridge, it looks exactly like the wards I've spent the last weeks in.

We don't come across anyone, though I suspect Beth's friend Soren has a lot to do with that. I want to believe the recruiters deserve what Soren did to them, but after meeting Aiden and knowing for a fact there are good people working in this place, I find it hard.

A smile works its way onto my face when I see a large glass door up ahead, through which the moonlight shines inside. My thoughts are immediately propelled to thinking of being outside again, and it takes a whole lot of self-restraint to stop myself from running towards the door like a maniac.

Beth pauses before she opens the door outside.

'Everything okay?' I ask.

She nods. 'Just waiting for Soren.'

Dalton stands right behind us and I have to move to look around his massive form to see the space behind him. Soren approaches us at such speed and with such stealth I would've thought he were a ghost if I didn't know better.

When he gets to us he stops and nods for Beth to continue. She turns back to the door and opens it, sticking her head out to check the coast is clear.

One-by-one we leave the building and when I take in my first breath of fresh air I feel a rush of emotions. I'm so happy to be free of the hospital, but I still feel trapped by what they've done to me. The experience wraps around me like a dark and heavy cloak I can't remove, no matter how much I wish I could.

Kelsey hugs me tighter, a smile lighting up her face. I can see she feels the same relief I do to finally be outside again.

'Elle, come on,' Beth hisses.

I hadn't realised I'd stopped walking and the others are all way ahead of us now. I rush to catch up with them, feeling silly for being overwhelmed by the outside world. It's hard not to be after so long locked away from it.

I take one last look at the hospital that has held me prisoner for such a long time and feel an overwhelming sense of release as it disappears behind another building. We're free.

CHAPTER SEVENTEEN

Once we're several blocks away from the hospital Beth stops outside the front of a clothes depot. It's not nearly as large as the one I'd been to in East Hope and the windows out front are covered in a thin layer of dirt and grime.

Beth glances at Dalton and nods in the direction of the door. He walks up to it and steadily traces his finger along the door's frame, he places his hand just inside the outline, against the hard wood of the door and the area within his tracing disappears. He steps through the gaping hole he's created into the store and once his hand is removed from the space the wooden door reappears. A moment later he unlocks the door from the inside and swings it open to let us in.

'You guys need to change out of those hospital robes,' Beth says, motioning for Kelsey and I to go inside. Kelsey nods eagerly, rubbing her hands over the goose bumps that have appeared on her chilled arms. I don't even feel slightly cold, just tired and nauseous.

'Shouldn't we get rid of Kelsey's cuff? Surely they'll be tracking us on it now?' I ask, as we enter. The air in the place smells stale and I sneeze as the floating dust tickles my nose.

Beth takes a look at the cuff around Kelsey's wrist before shaking her head. 'No, it looks like they swapped hers out for a dud in the ward. I doubt this can even comm someone, let alone track her. There's no harm in ditching it though, just to be safe.'

I catch a flicker of concern in her eyes, before she masks it. 'You should change.'

I look down at the blue hospital gown. It's conspicuous as hell and I can't wait to be rid of it. 'Give me a minute,' I say, as I set off into the store.

I wander through the racks, quickly picking out a pair of jeans, a black tank and a sweater. I'm making my way to a change room when Kelsey dives out at me from under a rack of clothes, causing me to jump back and gasp.

'Got you!' she squeals, delightedly.

I laugh awkwardly and try to remember how to breathe again. She scared the hell out of me. I nervously glance at the front door, worrying she's made too much noise.

'Yeah, you got me, but now you need to get some clothes Kels.' She nods and looks back at the racks of clothing determinedly. 'Don't forget shoes and socks, and a jacket,' I call after her as she disappears into another rack.

Once I'm changed I meet the others by the front door. My body tingles with nerves. We're still close to the hospital and this place feels way too quiet. I want to put as much distance between that place and myself as quickly as possible.

'Where's Kelsey?' Beth asks.

'Here I am!' she squeals. She's wearing an old princess costume and standing in a pair of women's high heels with a man's fur coat draped over her shoulders.

Beth and I burst out laughing when I see her. Dalton and Soren, however, look thoroughly unimpressed.

'I'll fix this,' I say, to the others.

It's difficult to explain to Kelsey her outfit is impractical. I manage to budge her on changing the shoes and jacket, but she absolutely refuses to get out of the princess dress.

When we leave the store, Kelsey is beginning to drag her feet and rub her eyes tiredly, so I pick her up in my arms to carry her.

'Where's Will?' she asks, her mouth pulling wide in a yawn.

'I'm not sure, but he's with Ryan so I'm sure he's safe. We'll see if Beth can help us find him once we've stopped.'

Kelsey nods and closes her eyes. I walk slightly faster to catch up with Beth who is a few feet in front of us. 'Where are we going?' I ask her.

'I can't tell you the exact location, but it's somewhere you'll be safe from recruiters and those crazy doctors in the hospital.'

'Do you know what they were doing to us in there?'

She nods. 'Yeah, we know what they are up to, but I sure as hell didn't know you were involved. One day you were there, the next you were gone. I didn't know what to think.

'We couldn't get a read on your cuff. We tried to check for any trace of you at the hospital, but there was nothing. I even checked with our contacts to see if you'd been taken to the farms, but that was a dead end too. It was like you vanished into thin air, like you never existed.'

She sounds sad as she says this and I wonder if maybe she has cared about me all along. Maybe she'd been pushing me away because she wanted to protect me? I swallow tightly and struggle to push back tears.

'I'm sorry you had to worry,' I say.

She smiles. 'It doesn't matter. I'm just glad to have you back in one piece.'

I smile warmly back, though I don't feel like I'm in one piece. Not anymore. I feel like I've been broken, shattered into a thousand pieces of the person I once was. The things they did to me in there changed me and I feel like a shadow of the person I used to be. I don't even have control of myself without this band across my wrist. I can't tell Beth any of this though. I can barely admit it to myself.

Glancing at the inhibitor, I am filled with despair. The experiments the doctors performed on me have produced the wild talents that course through my body. The few I've managed to use have only hurt the people around me, and I'm terrified to find out what else might be lurking beneath my skin. Maybe Dr. Wilson's cure can stop my mutations from getting any worse? If so, we can't waste any time in finding it and we'll need Aiden out of the hospital to do so.

'How did you get involved in all this?' I ask Beth, trying to ignore my fears, which so easily rise to the surface of my mind.

She looks over her shoulder at Dalton and Soren who walk together several metres behind us, quietly talking to each other, before turning back to me. 'When I was taken I was only in East Hope for a matter of days before I was moved to the talented dormitories in the north. Back in those days, talents were still a relatively new concept and Hope was chaotic and a lot less ordered than it is now.

'There was still free movement between the different areas in Hope and I spent most of my time ditching classes trying to find Mum. During my search I met a man named M who knew things no one else here seemed to know. One of those things was Mum was dead.'

'I heard. I'm so sorry Beth,' I whisper, my throat closing up as I think of the same fate that awaits Kelsey, Will and me if we can't find a way to make the mutations stop.

'You can call me April,' she replies. 'We're among friends.' She clears her throat, focusing back on where we're walking. There are no lights on the street, but under the glow of the moon shining brightly above I can see her eyes are wet with unshed tears.

I look away from her face to the dilapidated townhouses that stand before us forming two long rows down the sides of the road. Their small front gardens are overgrown with weeds, no lights emanate from any of their windows and there's not so much as a whisper of sound on the street. This place feels truly abandoned and I feel like we could be the only people walking the surface of this earth right now.

'Once I found out she was dead, and how it happened because she was brought to the surface too soon, I was so angry,' April continues. 'I felt an unrelenting rage at the government here, with the council in the ARC and towards anyone who has ever had authority over me and has abused it. It felt like all these people ever did was take our choices away from us and I'd had enough.

'M could see how passionately I felt the injustice of Mum's death and he told me about his movement. It was small at first, but we've grown bigger and bigger. He showed me we didn't have to just sit by and do nothing. He showed me the truth about what Joseph and his government are doing.'

'What are they doing?' I ask.

'Joseph was never elected to be in charge,' April says, lowering her voice. 'He was given temporary control during the establishment of Hope, but he has taken matters into his own hands. The city was supposed to be a fresh start for everyone, but all he cares about is the talented.'

'Why?'

'He wants to control who is talented and who isn't. He's obsessed with heightening talents by making them stronger and more dangerous, but he also wants the power to take them away.'

'That's where the experiments come in,' I add.

'Yes,' she nods. 'He has the patients in the hospital and most people in West Hope being experimented on. He has even begun taking people from the ARCs prematurely because of his sick obsession. They are his guinea pigs.'

I think back to my trip to West Hope with Lara, when we saw how sick and helpless the people looked. How can he think it's okay to make people sick in such a way?

'We're different though,' April continues. 'While he's looking for a way to make himself more powerful, we're simply trying to get everyone above ground safely. But we won't be able to do that with him in charge.'

'How is he still in charge after the things he's done?'

Her eyes glint with silent anger. 'Because no one has stood up to him and with the recruiters following his every order, no one wants to.'

I shake my head. 'One man shouldn't have the power to determine how we rebuild our world.'

'No,' she agrees.

I fall silent as I allow her words to sink in. She's been through so much since coming to the surface. I had no idea the secrets she kept when I first arrived in Hope.

'What about the Masons? Is there a reason you've been living with them?' I ask.

April slowly nods. 'Paul Mason is Joseph's number two in charge and I've been placed with him to get inside information.'

'But they treat you like you're their daughter.'

'To Paul and Cathy I really am their child.'

'How is that even possible?' They act like a real family. I find it hard to comprehend how she could infiltrate a family at that level.

'Because of my talent,' she explains.

'Which is?'

She hesitates before she responds, like she worries I will judge her for what she is about to say. 'A form of mind manipulation,' she replies, quietly. 'I can manipulate people to believe whatever I want them to believe. With the Masons, I've manipulated them to the point where they believe I am their child.'

'Do they even have a daughter?'

'Yes, but the real Beth is still in the ARC. It was easy to slip into their family, to make them believe I was Beth and I had recently been taken from the ARC and brought here. I look pretty similar to the girl and am the same age.'

'Are things up here so desperate for you to pretend you're someone you're not and live as an imposter in their family?'

'Are you really asking me that after what you've just been through?' April falls silent and stops walking. She holds her hand out to the two behind us for them to stop too.

'We have to be quiet now, we're nearing the wall.'

I follow the direction of her gaze to the huge wall that stands at the end of the street. As I stare at the formidable structure, I notice how incredibly quiet it is—unnaturally so. I look over my shoulder before moving to follow April. The hairs on the back of my neck stand on end and my skin seems to crawl with each step I take. Something tells me we are being watched.

CHAPTER EIGHTEEN

M y eyes narrow as I watch the still street behind me, searching for anything prowling in the murky night. There's not even a wisp of air running through the tall grass that coils around the rusty fences of the houses on the street, and no movement to indicate someone might be there. It's as though the city is holding its breath in anticipation, like it can feel something is about to happen.

I turn and try to focus on the wall before us, but looking at it doesn't make me feel any calmer. It is foreboding in the darkness. It stretches far into the distance and reaches up high into the sky. It is all that separates us from the east of the city, but for most in the west this concrete barrier could be an ocean for all the luck they'd have at getting past it.

'Come on,' April whispers, motioning for us to follow her into its shadow.

Kelsey is sleeping in my arms and her body is growing heavy after carrying her for so long, but I refuse to let someone else take her. She's been through so much tonight and April is the only one I trust in this group of strangers.

When we get to the last building before the wall, April motions for us to hang back while Dalton continues towards it. When he gets there he draws a glowing outline on the thick concrete surface, just as he did in the hospital and the clothing depot.

When he presses his hand against the wall the concrete within the outline dissolves and a window appears through which we can see the glowing lights in the east of the city.

'He comes in handy,' I say to April.

'Tell me about it,' she replies. She checks the coast is clear before ushering us over to the window Dalton has created in the wall.

I feel unnerved as I walk out from the protection of the building and into the open space that leads up to the wall. I can't shake the feeling someone's out there and I keep waiting for a siren to go off or recruiters to descend on us. There's no sign of pursuit though.

As we near Dalton, I catch a flicker of light out of the corner of my eye.

'Get down!' Dalton roars.

I throw Kelsey and myself to the ground, not taking a moment to question the order. I try to create a cage with my arms to protect Kelsey with, and land on my side, rather than on her, but her body still slams hard against the ground. As we hit it, I feel a wave of hot air pass over the top of my body. As I glance over my shoulder a huge purple flame recedes from above us, back towards a man, who is high-lighted by the flickering embers of a fire that seems to curl and coil its way around his hands. A recruiter.

April crawls up to me and grabs my elbow, pulling me up. 'We need to get to the wall!' she says.

I scramble to my feet and drag Kelsey up with me, who has woken and begun to cry from our rough landing.

'Get to Dalton. Soren and I will distract him,' April says.

I grab Kelsey's hand, but she doesn't want to move, so I pick her up and run. My arms ache as I try to keep hold of her and my legs throb as I push them to run faster. My stomach churns with fear, and it's hard to ignore the overwhelming exhaustion I've felt over the last couple of hours as I push my body to its limits.

I check behind me as I run and see Soren and April both taking cautious steps back towards the wall as the recruiter moves in. The man's focus is almost entirely on Soren, flames whipping out from his body towards him, as though the long tendrils of flame were an extension of his arms.

'Elle!' Dalton yells, making me turn back to the wall. It's close now and I can see Dalton clearly in the darkness. 'I can't hold this open much longer, you need to get through!' he shouts, urging me to run faster.

By the time I get to him, Dalton's body is shaking, and his nose has started to bleed. He looks like he could collapse at any moment.

'What about April and Soren?' I ask.

'They'll come through once you're safe on the other side. *Go!*' he urges.

I duck under his arm to move through the gaping hole he's created. Shivers run down my spine and creep up my arms as I make my way through, disappearing as soon as I'm on the other side.

I wait for the others to come through. Kelsey is still crying, so I rub her back and make soft cooing noises to comfort her as I continue to watch their retreat.

April and Soren stand merely twenty feet from the wall now, ducking and diving as they avoid the burning whip of the recruiter's flame. Dalton looks even worse than he did a few moments ago, and as though he's read my thoughts, he staggers and the section of cement wall reappears, flickering back into existence, before disappearing again once Dalton steadies himself.

'April!' I scream, the terror in my voice causing her to face me. 'Dalton can't hold it any longer!'

She focuses on Dalton and what she sees causes her enough panic to grab Soren's arm and pull him into a run.

They race fast to get to the wall, and Soren's body seems to blur as he moves. He's the first one through and April is almost there when a huge flame rises up behind her.

'Watch out!' I yell.

She dives through the window with Dalton hurling his body after her, just as the flame is about to engulf them. They land harshly against the hard ground, with the section of wall forming solidly back in place behind them. A wisp of smoke billows up from where the fire had been just moments ago.

'Are you okay?' I ask, rushing over to help April stand. Part of her jacket is singed, and there is an ugly red welt forming on her upper arm.

'I'm fine,' she says, ignoring the gravel scratches that are bleeding on her hands and the burn mark that looks incredibly painful.

I check the other two. 'Are you guys both okay?'

Dalton groans an affirmative as he slowly rights himself and Soren gives a non-committal shrug, which I assume means he's fine. I am yet to hear a word from the man.

'We need to keep moving,' April says, slowly standing and not stopping for a moment to catch her breath. She pats the gravel from her arms and starts to move away from the wall.

'How did he find us?' I ask, following her.

'I doubt they knew who we were. It looked like it was a lone recruiter patrolling the wall and we just happened to be in the wrong place at the wrong time.'

'But he attacked. Surely that means something?'

She glances back at the wall, with a flicker of unease entering her eyes before she quickly dismisses it. 'He saw us opening a window through the wall to the east, that would have been reason enough for the attack. We got away, that's the main thing. We're heading this way,' she says, nodding her head in the direction of two tall buildings that mark the entrance to a cold and uninviting alleyway. Not even a sliver of the moon's light touches the narrow passage and it's impossible to tell where it leads.

I hesitate by the entrance, where the dark fragments of shadow from the alley reach out to the moonlit street. 'Where are we going?' I ask April.

'To the south side of the city,' she says, not hesitating as she continues into the darkness of the alley.

I race to catch up with her, ignoring the short spike of unease that rushes through me as I enter. 'But I thought no one lived there.'

'That's because it's what we want people to believe.'

'What do you mean?'

'We've put a lot of time into creating a place the world here doesn't want to know about. I can explain more when we get there, but we should hurry.'

She steps her pace up a notch and I struggle to keep up with her with Kelsey in my arms. I pat Kelsey lightly on the back of her head and slowly ease her to the ground.

'Do you think you could walk for a little bit?' I ask her.

She nods tiredly, but doesn't grumble. As her eyes adjust to the darkness, her small hand immediately seeks mine and she clasps it tightly, refusing to let it go.

We exit the alley, but then enter another, followed by another. Each is just as dark and empty as the last, and my unease only grows the further into South Hope we journey.

There are no lights illuminating any of the windows in the buildings we pass and the city becomes more and more neglected. Thick green vines creep across the ground and up and around the walls of buildings, creating an entangled prison for the stone structures. Weeds grow out of large cracks that interlace across the surface of the road and there are large gaping holes where the asphalt has sunk. The wrecked cars we pass, abandoned on the side of the road, are covered in patches of rust. This area is deserted and it's easy to see why no one lives here.

I become increasingly uneasy as we walk. The night seems darker here and the streets feel more dangerous, like anyone could be lurking around the corner waiting to pounce on us. The skin on the back of my neck tingles and the further we walk, the more I have to fight the urge to turn around and run in the other direction. I *really* don't want to be here.

I slow my steps until I've stopped completely. I peer over my shoulder to the road behind us. It looks safer in that direction and it fills me with a sense of warmth and comfort when I consider changing route. Maybe we're going the wrong way?

April touches my arm lightly, causing me to jump. 'You have to ignore the urge to turn and do a runner. We have a device that projects the unease you're feeling, to help discourage unwanted visitors.'

I glance at the foreboding road that rises up behind her. My insides turn cold, just by looking at it. 'Are you sure? It doesn't seem safe here.'

She smiles. 'Yes, I'm certain. I can feel the same urge to leave too, but you just need to ignore it. Don't worry, it will be fine once we're in camp.'

'We're going to a camp?' I ask. April nods in response.

'And we'll be safe there?' I glance at Kelsey next to me, hoping desperately I'm taking her to a place where she will be protected.

'We are never safe,' she says, softly. 'But for the time being, you should be.'

CHAPTER NINETEEN

The sun is slowly beginning to rise over the mountains in the far off distance when April announces we're nearly there. We must have been walking for hours by now and in the cool morning light I can just make out where we have been brought.

'This is it?' I ask, peering around.

We have reached the edge of the city and sprawling out before us is an expanse of long grass rippling gently in the breeze. In the distance, beyond the grass, is a tall barbed wire fence, but I'm unable to see what it borders.

As we move closer, I am immediately struck by an array of strange, vile smells, which emanate from the area. I crinkle my nose in disgust. The ground beneath my feet isn't any better. Rather, it consists of thick, gluggy dirt that slurps and sucks at my shoes, which easily sink into it.

April leads the way. She moves certainly, following a path that avoids the large pools of water that collect on the sludgy ground. But even on the route we're taking, my shoes and the bottom of my pants are still covered in mud.

'Is this where you were that night when I caught you sneaking in?' I ask April. She'd been defensive when I'd asked her where she'd been at the time, and I remember wondering at the mud that caked her shoes.

She nods. 'I only come here when absolutely necessary, though I've more and more reasons to lately.'

'Why?'

'You'll see once we arrive. There's someone who will be *very* happy to see you,' she says, winking at me cryptically.

My eyes light up and I lightly grab her wrist. There's only one person she could mean. 'Sebastian. Do you have him here?'

She gives me a small smile. 'Yes, he's at camp.'

I try to fight a responding smile and fail badly as I all but beam at the thought of seeing him again. Could I really be seeing him so soon?

We continue through the marshland, which only becomes more difficult to navigate. Kelsey struggles to walk without slipping and the hem of her princess dress drags through the mud, quickly becoming coated in dirt. No matter how much I try to help her she still continues to fall.

She looks miserable and on the brink of tears, but doesn't let one escape. Even when her lower lip trembles, and I think she's about to cry, she tightens it, scrunches her lips up in a pout and pushes on. I have to admit I'm impressed by how strong she's acting, especially given how tired she is after such a long night.

When we reach the edge of the marsh, we approach an old barbed wire fence. The wire sags heavily in sections and is covered in rust. Behind the fence is a large open concrete lot that surrounds a series of huge warehouses made from corrugated iron. The whole place seems more abandoned than the camp I imagined April had been talking about.

April lifts the corner of one piece of loose fence and motions for us to crawl under it while she holds it back. Dalton goes first, and I'm surprised he's able to fit through the small gap, but he does so easily. Soren is next, then Kelsey.

When it's my turn to go, I clamber my way under the fence, my shirt catching on the wire and tearing. I huff out an exhausted breath as I stand and inspect the damage. It's only a small tear, so nothing to worry about. Kelsey resumes her grip of my hand.

'How are you holding up?' I ask, crouching down to look her in the eyes.

'I'm okay,' she says, stifling a yawn. 'I didn't like the mud.'

'No, me neither. I think we're nearly there now, so we can have a rest soon.'

She nods, yawning again. 'I think I'd like that.'

'Me too.'

I stand and watch as April manoeuvres under the fence easily with well-practiced movements that look like they've been done many times before. She nods her head at the large sheds. 'We go that way,' she says, taking up her position in the lead again.

We walk across an open space towards the buildings. The place feels empty with no towering buildings nearby and no life to be seen. I feel like we're making our way across a dusty concrete desert.

When we get to the first huge building, which stands out in the middle of nowhere, we don't go inside. Instead, April directs us to the next one, which lies beyond it.

A man stands in the doorway of the second building, and though he's far away I recognise him immediately. 'Sebastian?' I whisper, my heart stilling and the corners of my eyes filling with happy tears.

He turns, as though I'd shouted his name, and on seeing me a huge grin covers his face. I squeal when a moment later he has disappeared from the doorway in the distance and reappears in front of me.

He doesn't say a word as he takes one step to close the distance between us and pulls me up in a massive bear hug. My body fits perfectly within his arms, and a sense of feeling whole again fills me.

'Are you trying to crush me?' I say, with a laugh, after a minute of being held in his iron grip. He pulls back and, as he does, I notice April watching us closely, a calculating look in her eyes.

'I'm so glad you're okay,' he says, the look in his eyes changes and the happy sparkle in them disappears, being replaced by a look of pain. 'Everything that has happened to you is my fault. The bridge ... I wasn't strong enough to take you with me, and I was already on the other side of the river before I realised you were left behind. I'm sorry Elle.'

'You're not to blame for what happened to me,' I tell him. I take his hand in mine and give it a squeeze. 'I would never blame you, it wasn't your fault.'

'Seb, we'll have plenty of time for you to apologise later,' April interrupts. 'Elle and Kelsey need to get settled. They've both had a long night.'

'Sorry April,' Sebastian says, rolling his eyes and smiling. 'It's like she thinks she's the boss of me,' he whispers, before taking a step away from me.

'I heard that,' April says, 'and that's because I am.'

April glances at Kelsey whose head is slumping tiredly as we walk towards the building. 'Do you want me to carry her the rest of the way?' she asks me.

I nod, feeling too exhausted to resist the offer and carry her myself. I couldn't do it now even if I wanted to. I'm tired and my body feels heavier with each step I take. I almost wish someone would carry me too.

Sebastian lightly touches my arm, causing me to pause as the group continues on ahead of us. 'How are you feeling?' he asks. The serious look in his eyes is back.

'I've been better, but I've also been worse.'

'I heard what they were doing to you in there,' he says, his eyes growing darker. 'I spent every day of the last two months trying to find you and would've stormed the place myself if I'd known you were there. But by the time I was told April had gone to get you, you were already out.'

I give him a small smile. I have no doubt he would've taken everyone in the hospital on if he'd known I was there. 'I'm glad you weren't put in danger. They have inhibitor sensors everywhere in the hospital and you would've had a hard time getting me out by yourself. Sending April and her team was best.'

'Still...' He leaves the word hanging in the air before drawing up straighter and trying to push the pain in his eyes away. We slowly catch up with the others.

'How did you end up here?' I ask Sebastian, trying to change the conversation.

'When I got to the other side of the river, I was exhausted from using my talent. I tried to get back to you, but I was completely drained and the effort caused me to black out. By the time I woke up it was morning and I was here.'

'But how?'

'When you surfaced and told me Seb was in Hope I searched for him,' April says, slowing her steps to join us. 'But I didn't want him to get involved in what I was doing. I didn't want to put him in danger, and so I thought it would be best if he were left in North Hope. We have people monitoring the recruiter's database. When you went there and escaped with Seb, his profile was flagged by them. They wanted him captured at all costs, so I knew I didn't have a choice anymore. He had to be brought in.'

We enter the building through the doorway I'd seen Sebastian standing in before. Three massive planes, which take up most of the area, are inside. They look like large birds of prey with flat angled wings and sharp pointed beaks. I can almost imagine them hovering in the sky, ready to drop down on their prey. They would move with such speed and precision, the target wouldn't even know they were coming.

The whole wall on the other side of the room has been cut out and huge doors are folded at the edges. Morning light spills in through the large, open entrance, highlighting the sheer size of the building.

'What is this place?' I ask April.

'It used to be an air force base, but I don't think anyone's been here since impact. Well, anyone but us that is.' She leads me past the winged beasts and out through the large opening on the other side of the building. It's just as open and deserted on this side of the hangar, and there's no sign of any camp.

I begin to worry we're nowhere near to getting there. My legs are exhausted and I feel close to dropping. I don't know how much longer I can walk for.

'How much further is it?' I ask.

'We're nearly there,' April replies. 'Make sure you remember the route we're taking. If you ever come or go from camp the alarm will be raised if you don't come through the second hangar we just came out of.'

'There are people watching us?' I ask, searching for any sign of life in the open ground around us.

'Yes, we always have people on look out,' April says. I look around again but can't think where they could be watching from.

We follow a faded yellow line painted on the concrete over towards thick trees and bushes, which grow wildly along the edge of the open concrete area. Just beyond the treetops I catch sight of a shimmer in the air. I haven't seen The Sphere that protects Hope so clearly before. The camp must be right by the edge of it.

As we enter under the canopy of trees, April turns to me. 'Welcome to our camp,' she says, a bright smile on her face. I peer over her shoulder, unable to make out more than bushes and trees. As my eyes adjust I can slowly see a small city of tents appear, which have been expertly camouflaged into the surrounds.

It's uncanny how well the camp has been hidden in amongst the trees and bushes. I could easily walk past the camp without realising it was there.

'Come on, I'll show you where you're sleeping,' April says.

The camp is quiet at this time of the morning, and everyone appears to be sleeping as we make our way past the rows of tents. I can hear soft murmurs coming from some tents and a few snores coming from others.

'We put four to a tent, but for the moment we'll just keep it to you and Kelsey until you've recovered,' April says. 'There are a couple of families based with us. Once you're settled we can put Kelsey in with them if you'd prefer?'

'No, I want to stay with her.' I stumble and reach out to grasp Sebastian's arm next to me.

'You okay?' he asks.

I take a moment to steady myself. 'Yes, sorry. I haven't walked this far in a long time and I'm still not feeling one hundred percent.'

'Here.' He puts one arm around me to help support me as I walk, and I try to ignore the way my heart leaps at his touch.

'Thanks.'

Soren and Dalton move to part ways with us.

'We'll be briefing M in one hour, make sure you're at the control tent by then,' April calls after them.

Dalton nods and Soren gives a dismissive wave of his hand as they disappear behind a tent and venture into the bushes.

April leads us to a cluster of tents a little further away than the others. There are 8 tents grouped together in the section and they seem a little smaller than the ones we'd walked past earlier.

Sebastian stops by the front of the first one we pass. 'Will you be okay?' he asks, slowly lowering his arm from around my waist, as though he's reluctant to let go.

I nod.

'She'll be fine Seb, she's only next door,' April says.

Despite April's words, he still looks hesitant to leave. 'I'm just in here if you need anything. I'll leave you to rest,' he says, before entering his tent.

April moves to the next tent and unzips the opening. Inside is a small space that houses two sets of bunk beds. Kelsey is firmly asleep in April's arms, and April gently places her down on the bottom bed of one of the bunks.

'There are some fresh clothes in the trunk over there, and there's a small stream just beyond the trees behind the tent if you need to clean up. Don't worry about the mud on the sheets,' she says, still looking at Kelsey who lies there in the princess dress she dragged through the mud. 'It's better she gets some rest rather than wake her up now.'

'Thanks,' I reply, feeling a rush of gratitude. April risked so much for us tonight. I don't know where to begin to properly thank her. 'I have so many questions...'

'There will be plenty of time for answers later. You should get your rest now.'

I nod at Kelsey. 'She was getting treatments in the hospital too, and recently had a bad reaction to it. I want to get her checked out.'

April's face looks grave. 'We have some of the best doctors on the surface here. If anyone can help her *and* you, it will be them.'

She goes to leave, but I touch her arm causing her to pause. 'Do you know someone named Ryan? He managed to get my friend Will out of the hospital when we initially tried to escape. They teleported out, but didn't return. I need to know what happened to them. Can the people here help me find him?'

She looks surprised at what I've said. 'You know Ryan?'

'Yes. I've known him since I was in the ARC. Why? Do you know him?'

'Yes,' she responds slowly, I can hear the hesitation clearly in her voice. 'But I don't know anything about earlier tonight or about your friend Will. Ryan isn't exactly a part of our group here, but I'll see what I can find out for you.'

My shoulders slouch with relief. 'That would be great, thanks.'

'Now, I'll see you in a few hours,' April says, zipping the door of the tent closed behind her. 'Get some rest,' she calls, as she moves away.

I quickly change into the fresh pants and top April gave me, then slump onto the bed. I want to sleep more than anything, but I can't stop replaying the night's events in my mind. We may be finally out of the hospital and away from their experiments, but the inhibitor on my wrist is a reminder I'm still not free.

CHAPTER TWENTY

April stands by the entrance to our tent, pulling back the opening to allow the bright midday sun to spill into the room. Her dark hair appears lighter in the sunlight and she seems more at ease than she was last night.

'Are you both ready to go? I need to take you to see M now,' she says.

Kelsey and I shuffle slowly to the entrance. I feel shattered after last night and Kelsey must be even more exhausted. 'Yeah, we're ready,' I reply.

'Would you like to go play with some of the other children?' April directs her question to Kelsey, who takes a step closer to me and grabs hold of my hand. She shakes her head.

'Can she come with us?' I ask.

'I don't see why not,' April responds.

The rest of the camp is awake now, and no one seems to take any notice of us as we move past the other tents. Everyone here is purposeful as they go about their daily tasks and there's a sense of resolve and quiet tension to the place.

'Were you able to find anything out about Will and Ryan?' I ask, as we walk down a thin dirt pathway that cuts between two tents.

She refuses to meet my gaze. 'Yes, but I'll tell you about it after we've talked with M.'

'Did something bad happen? Are they both okay?' Her inability to look at me has me jumping to bad conclusions.

'They're fine ... let's just wait until after the meeting to talk about them. Okay?'

I frown and chew on my lower lip as I silently follow her. Something bad must have happened. Seeing as Ryan didn't return for us, it's the most obvious explanation. I try not to worry, but how can I not? If anything, her words have me more concerned than I was before.

The large tent April takes us to is abuzz with activity, and seems to be the nucleus from which the rest of the camp operates. People rush in and out of the opening, and within the tent the faces of its inhabitants are all calculating and grave.

There are a series of long tables, some of which are covered in piles of paper, while others hold computer screens and high-tech looking gadgets.

April pushes past the men that crowd around one of the screens and leads us to the back of the tent. Not one of them gives us a second look and they all appear fully absorbed in what they're doing. Once we make it to the canvas wall at the far end of the tent, April pulls it back, to reveal a smaller tent, connected to this one.

A weedy looking man stands inside staring intently at the screen on his lone desk. He looks like he's in his late thirties or early forties, though from the tired rings under his eyes he could easily be younger. His arms are crossed over his chest and there is such a look of intense contemplation on his face, he looks like he carries the weight of the world on his shoulders.

After a moment of waiting for him to acknowledge us, April clears her throat to announce our arrival and he finally looks over.

He smiles grimly at April and nods, before setting his startling purple eyes on me. The colour shocks me. I've seen purple tinted eyes up here before, but nothing with this kind of intensity. They remind me of the Lysart streaked clouds over the ARC after a storm.

'You must be Elle,' he says.

'Yes,' I reply.

'It's nice to finally meet you, I'm M,' he says, holding his hand out to me.

I take his hand in mine, but the contact causes a static shock to zap between our palms and I drop his hand quickly. He frowns and places his hands in his pockets as he returns to his desk and takes a seat behind it.

'Please,' he says, gesturing for us to sit in the chairs opposite him.

I sit on one and allow Kelsey to clamber onto my leg to sit on my lap. April remains standing in the background.

'I'm glad to see April was able to retrieve you both. She informed me of your disappearance weeks ago, though we had no luck in finding you. It's strange they had you in the hospital because the test subjects there are always from West Hope.' His eyes examine mine closely, as though searching for answers.

'I was never tainted. I escaped from the ARC,' I say. 'They told me my cells are mutating too quickly and it's killing me. That's why I was there.' My skin grows cold as I consider my fate and I glance down at my hands that restlessly pick at my nails.

'You're not dying,' he responds.

It takes a moment for his words to register and my eyes slowly lift to look into his. 'What do you mean?' I ask. My words are quiet, almost breathed rather than spoken.

'Whatever they told you in there, you're not dying. None of the kids in your ward were.'

'But we're all so sick...'

'That's because of their experiments. Initially your cells were mutating too quickly, but you adjusted to the extreme mutations and survived the change. It's rare, but that's exactly why they were interested in you and the other children in the ward in the first place. You all came to the surface too early, but survived. You were prime candidates for their experiments.'

'So, Kelsey and I aren't dying?' I try to come to terms with his words. I knew the hospital had been covering up secrets, but I never thought to question what they'd told me about the mutations that were happening to me. Especially when my memories returned and I could recall Sebastian's mum had died from the same thing.

A part of me feels relieved, but another part of me worries. They've done something to each of us, something our bodies weren't meant for, and I don't believe for a second I'll be coming out of this unaffected.

M nods. 'You will both be fine. Our contact Aiden went to a lot of trouble to get you out of the hospital. He told me they were taking a lot of interest in you there. That you were special,' M continues.

'Yes,' I respond, suddenly fearing what it is that M wants with me.

'Why are you special to them?'

'I'm not certain,' I respond. 'I guess they did more tests on me than the others, and Aiden tried to briefly explain. Something about being vital to their research,' I shake my head. 'I still don't fully understand.'

M smiles. 'Aiden told us about the tests they were running on you and about your talent. That's one of the reasons I was willing to send a team.'

A sudden flush of heat crawls up my neck and I try not to drop my gaze from his. 'What do you intend to do with us?' I ask, keeping my voice steady as I attempt to hide the fear I feel inside. Surely April wouldn't bring me here if she knew M intended to continue testing on me, but that's the exact feeling I get as M eyes me clinically.

'Of course, I don't mean to continue the tests they were doing in the hospital, our goals here are quite different. I hope you will help us though.'

'With what?'

'If Aiden is right, your body appears to adapt and replicate talents when injected with them. The doctors in the hospital were preoccupied with trying to figure out a way to use your talent as a means for giving others talents. I, however, believe this talent for adaptation could be vital to finding a way to help the people in the ARC return to the surface.'

'You think that's possible?' I ask, thinking of the cure Dr. Wilson has supposedly developed. I want to tell M about it, but something stops me from saying anything to him.

'Yes, but we will need your cooperation.'

'What do you want me to do?'

'I'd like for you to visit our doctors in the medical clinic. They'll be able to give you a better idea of what will be required. Will you help us?'

I hesitate. As much as I want everyone from the ARC to return to the surface, I don't know if I'm brave enough to willingly accept more tests after the last few weeks of my life.

'Do you think my talent can help?' It still feels strange to talk about my talent out loud. I can still hardly believe I have it.

Something flickers across M's eyes and he glances up at April behind me, before focusing back on me. 'You beat the odds and survived the mutations that would kill most people who surfaced from the ARC too early. That fact alone could help our team. So yes, I think your talent will help.'

I sink down in the chair as I try to weigh the facts and make up my mind. 'I-I want to help...' my words hang empty in the air. I do want to help, but I also just want to be myself again. I don't want the constant tests, but am I so selfish I'd deny people a chance to return to the surface because of a few tests?

'Why don't I give you some time to consider this?' M says. 'You can let me know tomorrow morning what you've decided.'

I nod and go to follow April from the tent, but stop before I leave.

'Will someone be going back for Aiden? He was planning to leave the hospital with us and I'm worried about his safety in there.'

'I'll be looking into it,' M replies.

I doubt I'll get a better answer than that, so I nod and follow April.

Worry gnaws at my insides as I exit the tent. It seems like the only reason I was rescued is because M thinks I can help the people in the ARC. What if I refuse to help him? What will they put me through if I agree?

'I don't like him,' Kelsey whispers to me, once we're back outside. 'I got a bad feeling.'

'He's one of the good guys Kels. He will look after us. You'll see.' The words almost feel like a lie, and I worry that perhaps I've traded one prison for another. I shake my head, trying to distance myself from those thoughts. M has given me an option. He wants to help people in the ARC. He's not the bad guy here.

'Should we get some lunch?' April asks, brightly.

My stomach grumbles, but my eyes narrow on her. 'You were going to tell me about Will and Ryan,' I say, not fooled by her act.

The smile on her face drops and her face darkens. 'You'd better come with me.'

We follow her silently back through the maze of tents. Something feels off and I'm too afraid to ask her what's happened. I get the feeling I'm about to find out.

She leads us past the tents and further into the forest to a large shed beyond the edge of the camp. While it is camouflaged, like the tents, due to its size it is a lot easier to spot.

'What is this place?' I ask April.

'The medical clinic.'

I pause by the entrance, glancing down at Kelsey. 'Should she come in with us?' I ask, terrified of what's waiting for us inside.

'Yes, it should be fine.'

I relax, knowing Kelsey is allowed in. Things can't be so bad if she's able to come along.

April opens the door at the front of the building and leads us into a room that holds two rows of beds. Each bed has stark white sheets pulled tightly over it and the room feels similar to the children's ward in the hospital. It's not until my eyes reach the bed at the far end of the room that I finally see Will.

Kelsey's eyes light up and she squirms her hand out of mine once she sees him. She races down between the beds and jumps onto his bed and into his arms.

'Hey Kels,' he says, with a warm smile.

I jog down after her and sit on the bed next to Will, pulling him in for a large hug, once Kelsey has released him.

'I'm glad you're okay,' I say to him. I pull back and look at him closely. His skin is almost grey in colour and his lips are an unhealthy shade of blue. He looks so much worse than he did yesterday. Could it only be a day since I last saw him? 'What happened last night?'

His face drops and a look of pain crosses his features.

'Kelsey why don't you come with me?' April says. 'We can find some other kids for you to play with.'

'Can Will come too?'

'Maybe later,' Will says. 'I need to rest for now.'

Her face drops, but she follows April without complaint. As soon as they have disappeared through a door at the end of the room I turn to Will. 'What's wrong?'

He sighs. The sound more quiet and weary than I would have expected. 'As soon as Ryan teleported me here last night I collapsed. They say my body was convulsing uncontrollably and I was frothing at the mouth. I don't remember what happened exactly, but when I woke up I was here. I'm sorry Elle, it's my fault he couldn't get back for you in time.'

I take his hand in mine. 'Don't be silly. I'm just glad you're okay. Do the doctors here know what caused your reaction last night?'

'They're still looking into it, but from what they can gather my body is rejecting whatever they gave me in the hospital during their experiments and it's making me sick.'

I swallow tightly. 'Can they fix you?'

'I hope so,' he replies, a hint of fear in his eyes.

I glance over my shoulder to check if anyone is around before leaning in close to Will so no one else can overhear. 'Aiden thinks his grandfather has come up with a way for people to return to the surface without becoming sick.'

Will's eyes light up, but then he frowns. 'Who's Aiden?'

'A doctor who helped me escape the hospital when Ryan didn't return. I knew his grandfather in the ARC and he gave me a message for Aiden. Aiden thinks the message means his grandfather has a cure.'

'What sort of cure?' Will asks.

'From what I understand, the cure could stop people's genes mutating when they are overexposed to Lysartium. It would stop people getting tainted, so everyone can come above ground. Maybe it could help you?'

Will shakes his head. 'The doctors won't be certain what's wrong with me until they've done a full diagnosis. Who knows what they did to me in the hospital. Even if the cure could help, if his grandfather is in the ARC, surely getting his cure is impossible?'

'I don't know,' I reply. 'But I want to try.'

'So, what do we do?' he asks.

'I think I should tell M and see if he knows a way to get in contact with the ARC. Do you think he can help us?'

He pauses as he considers my question. 'I don't know.'

I sigh and rub my eyes tiredly. 'Kelsey has a bad feeling about him and after last night I'm beginning to trust any hunches she may have. April trusts him though, we *should* be able to trust him.'

'You don't seem certain,' he says.

'I don't know what to feel. After being in that hospital I don't know who to trust anymore.'

'You can trust me,' he says, smiling. His smile is shaken from his face though, as he violently coughs. I can feel the colour drain from my face as I watch him gasping for breath. He's worse than I thought.

'I know that,' I reply, when the coughing subsides. I try to hide the worry from my voice. He is obviously trying to be strong and doesn't want me to think he's sick, but something's definitely wrong with him.

'Are you okay?'

'I'm fine. Seriously, I'm not much worse than I was before. Plus, the doctors are working on fixing me here. I don't want you to worry about me.'

'I'm always going to worry about you,' I reply. He looks like he will argue with me, but instead sags into his bed. Our short conversation has taken a lot out of him.

'If you insist, but you have to let me worry about you too,' he says.

'I think that will be okay,' I reply. I notice a doctor standing down the corridor that leads from the back of the room, so I stand to leave Will's bedside.

'I'll be back to check on you in a bit,' I tell him.

He slowly nods. His eyelids are heavy and already half shut towards sleep. 'They keep rats here, you know?' he says, with a smile.

I smile back at him. 'You can show them to me later. I'm glad you're okay Will.' I'm not sure if he hears my reply as his eyes have drifted shut and he already appears to be sleeping.

I leave Will and walk over to the doctor. Seeing Will so sick has me worried and even though the idea of more testing terrifies me, not being able to help Will scares me more. If there's even the slightest chance my talent will help the doctors fix him, I have to help them out.

'Hi, I'm Elle Winters,' I tell the doctor, 'and I'm ready to start any tests M wants.'

CHAPTER TWENTY-ONE

I t's almost dark outside by the time I finish at the clinic. The doctors spent hours running a series of tests on me. Thankfully none of them were too invasive, but they still made me feel uncomfortable after what I've been through. When I'm released from the clinic for the day I feel a rush of relief. The doctors had been kind enough to me, but the clinic had felt a little too similar to the hospital for my liking.

I am slowly making my way back to my tent when I see a figure step out of the shadows of one of the trees.

'Ryan?' I ask, as he steps into my path. Even in the dim lighting I can see how tired he looks. There are bags visible under his eyes and he looks like he's aged several years since I last saw him.

'Hey Elle. I'm glad to see you got out okay,' he responds.

'Thanks to you. I don't know how you knew where to find me and what was going on, but I'd still be there if you hadn't come for me.'

'Some help I was. You should've been the one to come with me last night,' he replies, his voice thick with disapproval.

'No, I'm glad you took Will. I'm not sure he or Kelsey would've made it out if I'd gone first.' I try not to allow the weariness I feel right now to seep into my voice. He needs to know he did the right thing. 'How did you know? I mean, how did you manage to find me in the hospital? How did you even know I was in trouble?'

The more I think about it, the weirder it seems. I barely know anything about him and yet he seems to keep turning up to rescue me. He's clearly hiding things from me, but I have no idea what.

'It was only once the inhibitors were down that I could find you. Let's just say, I knew you needed my help.'

'What do you mean?'

He shakes his head. 'It doesn't matter, all that matters is you're here and you're okay.'

I sigh. Ryan's always been evasive; it's not surprising to find he hasn't changed. 'So, you're with these people...' I motion my hands back towards the camp. 'Do you live here?'

'No, on both counts.'

'Then what are you doing here? How do you even know where this camp is?'

'I have an understanding with M and I knew this was the safest place to bring you.'

'So it's safe here?'

'For now. I see you're wearing an inhibitor band,' he says, quickly changing the subject and nodding at the black device around my wrist.

I draw my wrist up to my chest and lightly touch the band, before pulling my sleeve down over it. 'Yes.'

'Have you tried to use your talents without it on?'

The way he asks me makes me pause. His voice is gentle and it's like he knows how terrified I am of taking the band off and hurting someone.

'You can't control them, can you?' he continues.

I slowly shake my head, which causes him to swear and start pacing. 'What's wrong?' I ask.

He swears again, so I reach out and touch his arm. 'Ryan?'

'It may already be too late,' he says, between his teeth.

I frown. 'Too late for what? I don't understand what you're talking about.'

'Your mutation is unique. It is always changing and the more talents you absorb and acquire, the more difficult you will find it to control yourself without that band.'

'There's nothing I can do to change what has been done to me,' I reply.

He stops pacing and grabs hold of both my arms. 'Promise me you won't let them give you any more talents.'

'I don't know why they would...'

'Damn it, Elle, promise me.'

'Okay, okay, I promise.'

His shoulders slouch and his arms drop from holding mine. I watch him closely, trying to understand why the hell he's acting so strange, but I can't figure him out.

'What would happen if they did—'

'You should focus on helping your friends find the cure,' he says, effectively cutting my question off.

'Well, we'd have a much better chance at finding one if Aiden was out of the hospital,' I grumble. 'I'm not even sure if M will help him. Is there anything you can do?'

Ryan's eyes darken. 'Aiden was the one who helped you when I couldn't come back, right?'

I nod. 'I'm worried something's happened to him because of helping me...'

'I'll try my best.' His cuff chimes and he glances down at it, then back at me. 'I have to go.'

Before I get the chance to respond to him, he disappears. There's no warning whatsoever, he doesn't even make a sound as he evaporates from sight. I feel cold after his departure and I find myself constantly looking at the inhibitor on my wrist as I return to my tent.

I can't figure out why he's concerned about my talent. What does he know that I don't? Why does he think it's too late?

When I get back to my tent I find Sebastian sitting on the ground out front of his, looking up at the sky above.

'Hey,' he says, as I approach.

'Hey yourself,' I reply, taking a seat on the ground next to him.

'I heard you agreed to more tests. How were they?' he asks.

I shrug. 'Tests are tests.'

He looks at me closely. 'If you ever want to talk about the hospital ... you know you can talk to me right?'

'I know,' I reply, with a smile. 'There's not much to say though. The place was a prison and they treated me like a lab rat. I survived. That's all there is to it.'

We sit in silence, and I pull my arms tightly across my body to warm myself from the chill in the evening air. I'd rather the chill biting into my skin though than the closed in walls of the hospital.

'What's that cuff you're wearing?' he asks.

'This?' I ask, lifting the inhibitor band up to show him.

He nods. 'You've been playing with it since the moment I saw you this morning.'

'Oh, I didn't realise. It's an inhibitor to make me normal. I can't control the talents they infected me with.'

'Can I see it?' he asks.

I jerk my wrist in close to my body. 'I can't take it off.'

'I wasn't going to, I just wanted a better look at it.'

'Oh, sure.'

He gently takes my hand and touches the device, lightly twisting it to look at it closer. 'Is it that bad?' he asks, looking up at me.

I try to reply, but the words fail to form in my mouth. I simply nod, though I can feel tears welling in my eyes. I quickly look away. 'They made me into a monster. They've broken me into a million pieces and the only thing holding me together is that stupid band around my wrist.'

Sebastian's hands go still around my wrist and I turn to look at him.

'You could never be a monster,' he says, his eyes focusing on mine. 'I know these talents you've been given are testing your limits, but I don't believe for a second they have left you broken. You will find a way to control them and you will be stronger for it.'

'I hope so,' I reply. I pull my wrist back from his hands and hold it in close to my body.

Sebastian shuffles closer to me and looking at him in the moonlight I am struck by the similarities between him and Ryan. They are both so protective of me, and it's good to feel like I'm not alone.

'Do you trust them?' I ask Sebastian. 'The people here in this camp, I mean.'

'April does,' he replies.

'I'm not asking if she does, I want to know what you think.'

'Yes, I think they can be trusted. Not once has anyone tried to use me for my talent.'

'Did they do that in North Hope?'

He nods. 'Every morning I was subjected to tests and hours of drills to improve my talent.'

'I thought you liked it there.'

'I did at the time. The afternoons were spent relaxing with the other students and if you stuck to the rules it was a pretty nice lifestyle.'

'Are you sad you left?'

'Not one bit. If I had stayed there I wouldn't have seen April again and I wouldn't be able to see you. I definitely wouldn't be able to do this...' He looks me deep in the eyes and slowly draws closer. Taking a measured breath he leans forward to kiss me.

I want to lean towards him too, but instead I draw back. 'I can't,' I whisper.

He frowns and pulls back himself. 'I thought you wanted this ... us?'

I look away, out into the darkness of the trees opposite us. For such a long time Sebastian was my world. I gave up my entire life in the ARC and risked everything to find him. He had been everything I wanted, he is everything I want, but right now I can't handle it.

'I don't know what I want right now,' I say, my voice so quiet it's almost a whisper. 'I want to feel whole again and I want to help find this cure.'

'But me?'

I glance up at him. His face is blank of emotion, but I know him well enough to know he's putting up a wall to cover how he feels. 'Just give me some time. I have a lot going on right now. Things I need to focus on if I'm ever going to feel like myself again.'

'Right,' he says, his voice dipping low. 'Whenever you're ready, I'll be here waiting. Until then ...' He holds out his hand to shake mine, which makes me laugh. Instead I pull him in for a hug.

'I would wait forever for you,' he whispers, softly into my hair. When he pulls back he smiles. 'I should go,' he says. 'You've had a long day and I'm sure you need to get some rest.'

'Yeah, I'm pretty tired,' I admit. 'I'll see you tomorrow.'

I stand at the same time as he does and watch him as he walks to his tent. He gives me a quick smile before he closes and zips the entrance shut.

I sigh and slowly traipse the last few steps to my own tent. Kelsey is fast asleep inside with April curled up next to her. I zip the opening shut silently and find my way to my own bed.

I crawl onto the lower bunk and lie back, staring at the slats of the bed above me. My body feels exhausted, but my mind is wide-awake as a million different thoughts fight for my attention. I need to help Will. I need to find out if Dr. Wilson has a cure. But the thought that keeps me awake is: what stopped me from kissing Sebastian? Why is that too much for me right now?

CHAPTER TWENTY-TWO

I wake to a strange fluttering feeling against my cheek. When I peek one eye open I can see the top of Kelsey's head, her face pressed up against mine.

'What you doing Kels?' I ask.

'I'm giving you kisses,' she responds. The fluttering feeling against my cheek continues and I'm fairly certain she's simply blinking her eyelashes against it.

'I'm not certain you're doing it right,' I respond, groggily.

She giggles. 'Of course I am. They're butterfly kisses silly.'

'Ohhh,' I reply. 'Butterfly kisses. I thought butterfly kisses where like this!' I grab a hold of her stomach and pull her down next to me to tickle her. 'Is this how butterflies kiss?' I ask, tickling one side of her tummy.

'No!' she squeals.

'How about this?' I tickle the other side.

'Nope!' she squeals, between giggles.

'Hmm, maybe it's like this!' I tickle both sides of her tummy and she wriggles around squealing with laughter. When I finally stop, we're both puffing for breath.

'I give up!' I say. 'I don't think I'll ever learn to do it right.'

'Maybe next time,' Kelsey says, seriously.

I stand and look over to the bed Kelsey and April slept in last night. It's empty.

'Did April say where she was going?' I ask her.

'She had to leave camp to go to school,' Kelsey replies, shuffling across the bed to jump off and stand next to me.

'Back in East Hope?'

Kelsey shrugs.

'Did she say when she'd be back?'

She ponders my question. 'Maybe later.'

I consider our options. We hadn't exactly been given a schedule for what to do with our time here, and I don't think the doctors will need to see me again so soon, but maybe a trip to the medical centre would be a good idea.

'Should we go visit Will?' I ask.

'Yeah,' Kelsey says, a big grin forming on her face. She can barely contain her excitement at the thought of seeing him again. I can barely contain my dread. What if we get there and he's become worse?

We quickly get ready to go and are barely out of the tent when Sebastian comes running over to us from the main area of the camp. 'I'm glad I caught you. You're needed in the control tent straight away. M wants to see you.'

'We were just going to see Will.'

He shakes his head. 'He'll have to wait. M wants to see you now. I think it's important.'

'Oh, okay.' I glance down at Kelsey who holds my hand.

'I can take her?' he suggests.

'Yeah, that would be great.' I crouch down so I am eye level with Kelsey. 'We can go see Will later. I need to see M first, so Sebastian will look after you for a while.'

'Okay,' she responds, as Sebastian takes her by the hand.

THE CONTROL TENT is a flurry of activity this morning, though I doubt this place ever slows down. I wonder at what they're all doing in here, they all seem so serious. I'll have to ask April about it once she gets back. As soon as I'm inside a woman directs me to M's office at the back of the tent.

'Thank you for coming,' M says, as I enter. April is already here and seated at one of the chairs facing his desk.

'I thought you were at school?' I ask April, as I take a seat next to her

She shakes her head. 'Didn't get a chance. I have my teachers there manipulated, so I won't be missed.'

M eases himself into the seat opposite us and I glance between him and April, attempting to gauge what the urgent matter could be. April seems as oblivious as I am. 'What's wrong?' I ask M.

'The recruiters have raised an alert. They're looking for you,' M replies.

I'm not exactly shocked by the news. 'Shouldn't we be expecting that?' I ask.

'Yes, it was to be expected, but what's problematic is they've placed you as a level one target. They think you're crucial to their research into giving people talents. They will stop at nothing to get you back.'

I look at April and can see the worry on my face reflected in her eyes. This sounds bad.

'Do they know about this place? Do they know I'm here?' I ask, turning back to M. The thought of being found and taken back to the hospital has me panicked. I can't go back there.

'No,' he responds. 'But I think it's important we train you to use your talents so you can defend yourself.'

His suggestion surprises me, but I already know how I feel on the matter. 'I don't want to learn to use them.'

'Elle, you have to,' April says.

'You don't understand. They're too powerful and I can't control them. I'll only hurt people if I let them loose.'

April looks to M and I can see her eyes pleading him to convince me, but he gives a small shake of his head and faces me. 'I won't force you to do anything, but you will be more likely to hurt people if you don't learn control. Just think about it for me.'

M goes silent, as he allows his words to sink in.

'Okay, I will,' I respond, standing to leave. 'Was there anything else you wanted to talk to me about?'

He shakes his head. 'You can go.'

APRIL WALKS with me out of the control tent. 'I could help with it, you know,' she says. 'I can use my talent to make you believe you know how to control your talents. You wouldn't be helpless. You wouldn't be out of control.'

'Would that even work?' I ask.

'It would have to be worth a try,' she says. 'The control of your talents is all in your mind. You don't believe you can control them, they scare you and you think they're too much for you to handle, so they will be. If I tap into that and change those beliefs, you should manage control over them.'

'Have you tried it before?' I ask.

'Well, no,' she says. 'But, for most people their talents come naturally and develop gradually. They slowly adjust to them over time. You've been plunged in the deep end, especially since they inhibited them the entire time you had them.'

I focus on the dirt path ahead of us and try to honestly consider what she's offered. I fear my talents and I want to refuse her without giving it a second thought. I've seen the damage they can do, and I have no idea what else they forced upon me in their experiments. I don't feel ready to attempt to use my talents again. Not after what I did to those men in the hospital.

How can April trust me to use them without hurting anyone, when I can't even trust myself? The thought alone is enough to make me sweat.

April lightly touches my wrist. 'Please, just let me try with you this once?'

I hesitate.

'I could take you away from the camp. Somewhere you won't be close to anybody else and you won't be able to hurt anyone. If it doesn't work, I won't bother you about it again.'

'Ok,' I find myself saying, much to the surprise of April and myself. 'But just this once.'

SHE TAKES me to one of the large plane hangars that we passed on our arrival. The huge building is almost empty inside, but for a few old and rusted plane engines that sit against one of the walls.

April leads me to the centre of the room where she sits down on the floor, directing me to do the same.

As I sit, I feel nervous. What if something goes wrong? What if it goes right and I find out about talents I possess that maybe I don't want?

'People struggle most with their talents when they are emotional. They lose their ability to focus on what they're trying to do and the talent ends up controlling them, rather than the other way around,' April says.

A wave of calm rushes over me and I feel a building sense of confidence and excitement at what we're about to do. 'Are you doing that?' I ask her.

She nods. 'Yes, I've manipulated your mind so you believe you can do it, which will help keep you in control of your fear.'

I smile. 'I feel great. Should I take the inhibitor off?' I ask.

'When you're ready.'

I look down at the black glass that runs around my wrist. It takes little effort to push the negative thoughts that surface in my mind away and only focus on the task at hand. I know I can do this.

I slowly ease the band from my wrist and place it on the mat next to me, still within reach. I close my eyes and allow the feeling of my talents being set free to run through my body. I feel as if my body pulses to some beat that only it can hear. The hairs on my arms stand on end and my skin tingles. It feels good.

'Deep breaths Elle.'

I take a long breath through my nose and out through my mouth.

'I want you to focus on each of your different senses. First, put all of your attention on your sense of smell.'

I think about what I can smell, but it doesn't seem any different to normal. I can't seem to smell anything unusual or anything with intensified strength. I'm grateful though. I'd seen a guy who was featured on the show Talented, who had a heightened sense of smell, and he could smell a rotten banana in a bin over a block away. Gross.

'My sense of smell is normal,' I say.

'Are you sure?'

'Pretty certain.'

'Okay, how about your hearing.'

As soon as she mentions the word, 'hearing,' and I begin to concentrate on it, the sounds in the room become magnified. Simple things, like April's breathing, become incredibly loud. It sounds like her mouth is pushed right up against my ear as she draws her breaths in and out.

It's not just the sounds in the hangar though. As I concentrate harder, other noises seem to fight for my attention. I can hear footsteps outside. One foot sounds like it's dragging more than another. Beyond that, I can hear the sounds of a bird's wings beating in rapid succession. I feel like I could hear a pin drop at the entrance to the hangar at the moment.

'Elle?' April thunders. My eyes squint in reaction. I swear I can feel the vibrations of the sound in the air.

'Yes,' I whisper, so quietly I doubt April can hear it.

'Open your eyes and focus on what you can see.'

I open my eyes and focus on my sight. The sounds around me become quieter, the longer I concentrate, but my vision appears to be normal.

'Everything's normal,' I say.

'Have you tried looking at any details?'

'Like what?'

She stands and walks to the far side of the room, about twenty feet from where I sit. 'What is the symbol on my earrings?' she asks.

I lean forward slightly and tilt my head as I look at one of her earrings. The small silver stud is simple, but it has a faint outline of a flower across its shiny surface.

'There's a flower on it,' I say. 'But anyone could see that. Couldn't they?'

She smiles but doesn't respond as she returns to sit opposite me.

'You can put your inhibitor back on,' she says.

I have mixed feelings as I return the black glass device to my wrist. It had felt amazing to be free of it, but I also still desperately crave the security it gives me.

'You did well,' she says, beaming at me.

I look down at my hands, and smile. I didn't break anything or hurt anyone. Having April here really helped.

'So you have enhanced sight and hearing,' she says, 'but your sense of smell is normal.'

'How did you stop the rest of my talents from getting out of control?' I ask her.

'I didn't,' she responds. 'All I did was help you to keep your emotions in check. You did the rest.'

'I did?'

She nods. 'I think by totally focusing on one talent, the effect of the others is minimised. If you're happy to, we should do this once every morning, working through your different senses. As you become better, we can work towards moving quickly between each one and using more than one at a time.

'If it's ever too much you should focus on what you can smell. That's a safe place for you to be as it's not a talent.'

'What about the other talents?'

'Those we can slowly introduce and work on with time, but for the moment, I think your senses are a safe place to start.'

I nod in agreement. Enhanced sight and hearing can't hurt anyone, so I'm more than happy to focus on them.

'Is that training done for the day then?'

'Yep.'

'And we'll go again tomorrow?'

'Yes, I'll see you here after breakfast and we can train again,' she says.

We leave the hangar, and April looks in the other direction, off towards the wire fence that forms a barrier between the rest of Hope and us.

'I have to go,' she says. 'I need to put in an appearance at the Mason's or they'll worry.'

'Wait. Before you leave I want to ask you about Hunter and Lara. Have they been at school recently?' I ask.

'No they haven't, not for a while at least. They both disappeared around the same time you did. Given their talents, and the amount of recruiter visits at school at the time, I assumed they'd been recruited.'

'I don't think they have been. Guards at the Reintegration Centre took Lara away and I have a bad feeling about Hunter. He went missing in North Hope while we were searching for Sebastian. Could you look into it for me?'

'I'll have a chat with M to see if he can check their records. It's likely they're in the north. They're both too talented to be placed anywhere else. They wouldn't waste talents like that.'

'When will you talk to him?' I ask.

'I'll be back here tomorrow. I'll have a chat to him after our training session.' She takes a few steps backwards as she moves to leave. 'Don't get into too much trouble while I'm gone,' she says, with a wide grin, before turning to begin her trek to East Hope.

I naturally smile back. It feels good to have her back in my life. To understand the reasons why she held me at arms distance to begin with. She was protecting me and I like to think I'd do the same for her.

I walk towards the medical centre to visit Will. I can't wait to tell him about what I achieved this morning. My only hope is he's feeling better today than he was yesterday.

CHAPTER TWENTY-THREE

The next few days I fall into the semblance of a routine. In the mornings I train with April and I spend the afternoons in the medical clinic, either for more tests or visiting with Will. Each visit he seems to lose a little of his spark and I think he misses being outside, as he talks about it constantly. Sometimes Kelsey will come with me, but most of the time she's playing with a couple of other kids in the camp who are her age.

Sebastian seems to be keeping his distance from me. He's still his usual self and he's not avoiding me or anything. I just get the feeling he's giving me the space I asked for and, I have to admit, I'm grateful. There are so many parts of myself I can't control at the moment, and adding more emotions into my life is not a good idea.

I roll onto my back to stare at the slats of the bed above me. I twist the inhibitor band around my wrist as I gaze at them. I hate I'm so reliant on the thing, but I'm nowhere close to surviving without it. Despite April's help, I somehow managed to start a fire in the training hangar yesterday. It erupted from my hand with no warning and I still have no idea what I did wrong.

Kelsey wakes me from my thoughts by jumping on top of me.

'It's time to wake up!' she says.

I glance at the time on the new CommuCuff I was issued. 'You know it's six-thirty in the morning, right?'

'But the sun's up,' she says, pouting. 'I want to be up too.'

I had been enjoying lying here but, like Kelsey, I have struggled to sleep past five since getting out of the hospital. It's near impossible to get that early morning wake-up drill out of my system.

'April won't be around for my training this morning. Do you want to visit Will with me?' I ask her, as I sit up.

'Yep,' she responds. 'Can Sebastian come too?'

I smile at her question. She's been following him around every chance she gets. It seems as though she has a new crush. I just hope she doesn't find out how I feel about him. She doesn't seem to like the idea of sharing her 'boyfriends.'

'I think it might be too early for him,' I respond. I doubt he'll be up before nine. He likes his sleep *way* too much. 'Maybe next time?'

'Okay,' she responds, her small shoulders slouching. Her disappointment only lasts a few seconds though and her eyes light up with excitement. 'Can I bring Will my picture I made for him?' she asks.

'That's a great idea, why don't you go get it?'

Once we're dressed we make our way over to the medical clinic. We're almost there when I hear a series of terrified shouts coming from the front entrance.

My stomach drops.

'Kelsey, run back to the tents and find Sebastian. Do you remember how to get there?'

'Uh-huh,' she says, nodding.

'Okay, go quickly. I'll come find you once I know what's happening.'

As soon as Kelsey disappears from view, I race to the entrance, my heart pounding fast. I don't know what to expect. The lone voice I can hear screaming sounds alarmed and in terrible pain.

I round the corner and my feet shudder to a stop beneath me. 'Aiden?'

Aiden stands by the entrance to the medical centre shaking violently and yelling for help.

'Aiden, what's wrong?' I rush over to his side. 'How did you escape?'

'It's Jane...' he sobs.

I look around, but he's all alone out here. 'Aiden, who's Jane? Where is she?'

'She didn't tell me...' he says, between sobs.

'What didn't she tell you?' I grab a hold of his arm to support him. 'Aiden?'

'They ... they ...'

'They?'

He looks over my shoulder and his eyes lock on something behind me. 'Jane!' he yells, rushing past me. I turn to see Ryan standing behind us, cradling a woman carefully in his arms.

'Ryan? What's happened?' I ask, following Aiden towards the two of them.

'We need to get her inside,' he says, heading quickly for the medical clinic. I hurry in before him to hold the door open, so he can carry her through.

'We need a doctor!' Ryan shouts into the room.

He lays the woman gently down on one of the empty beds. Her skin is deathly pale and her lips are tinged blue. I can see her chest still rising and falling as she breathes, but it looks like she's struggling even to do that. Aiden stands beside me, staring at her hopelessly, his entire body shaking.

'What's wrong with her?' I ask him, but he doesn't respond. 'Aiden, do something!' I urge.

'Come on Elle,' Ryan says, taking my arm to lead me away, as a doctor rushes over. 'We need to get out of their way.'

He pulls me over to Will. I struggle to tear my eyes from the woman until the doctor pulls a curtain across to shield her from view.

Will, who has just been woken by the shouts in the hospital, sits up and rubs his eyes. 'What's going on?' he asks me.

'I have no idea,' I tell him. I look at Ryan. 'What happened to her?' I ask.

He takes my elbow and guides me to sit on the edge of Will's bed, while he takes a seat on the bed across from it. 'They caught her trying to escape with Aiden the night you got out. He tried to protect her and said it was all his doing, but they wouldn't listen. They locked him in a room and took her to trial a new experiment on her.'

'She will be okay, right?'

He hesitates. 'I don't know. She's become very sick and is getting worse.'

'What can I do to help?'

Ryan leans towards me and takes my hands. 'There's nothing you can do now. You have to let the doctors do their job.'

I stand, shaking my hands free of his and start pacing. 'Surely there's something...' I mutter.

'Why would they trial something so dangerous on her?' Will asks Ryan, anger filling his eyes like I've never seen before.

'Because they're animals,' I respond. 'They think they can treat people like they're nothing. They take away their choices and then subject them to things I wouldn't wish upon my worst enemy. It's inhumane.'

'Elle, you need to calm down,' Ryan says.

'You want me to calm down?' I say, my voice rising. 'How can I calm down when there are still *kids* left in *that* place? How can I calm down when innocent people are subjected to the tinkering hands of these idiots who think they can play God? How can I calm down when they've turned me into a monster and made Will so incredibly ill?'

I crumble onto the bed and start crying. I feel hands on my back and can hear both Ryan and Will making soothing noises beside me, but none of it helps. I feel so angry with the doctors in the hospital and Joseph who has masterminded such terrible things. How can anyone think the experiments they do in there are okay? How can we ever hope to stop them?

'There's nothing we can do, is there?' I say, quietly.

'It's okay Elle. No one expects you to save the world,' Will says.

'I don't want to save the world. I just want to protect the people I care about,' I reply. 'I don't want innocent people to be experimented on like I was.'

When the doctor finally draws Jane's curtain back, we slowly approach to check on her and see how Aiden is doing. There's a little more colour in her cheeks, but she still looks deathly pale.

'They're doing what they can to make her comfortable,' Aiden says, from the chair he sits in by her bed. He looks like he's aged ten years since I last saw him. His eyes are red-rimmed and puffy, and his fingernails have been chewed to the quick.

'Can I get you anything?' I ask him.

He shakes his head, his eyes still focused on Jane.

'What's wrong with her?' Will asks, peering at the young woman.

'She surfaced too early and the mutations are killing her,' Aiden responds, with detachment.

'She wasn't like us then?' I ask.

'No,' he replies. 'I should've gotten her out of that place sooner, but it wasn't until I read my grandfather's message I had any hope she'd survive outside the hospital walls. When the recruiters found me trying to escape with her...'

He puts his head down in his hands. 'Now, I'll be lucky if she has any chance of recovery at all. I'm worried it's too late.'

'It's not your fault,' Ryan says. 'There was no way you could know what they'd do to her.'

I glance between Ryan and Aiden, as I wonder what exactly the recruiters put Jane through. I can't bring myself to ask though, and I don't think Aiden could handle repeating it.

'Maybe there's still hope...' He stands up and for the first time since I've seen him today there's brightness in his eyes that wasn't there before. 'We need to get in contact with the ARC. Whatever cure my grandfather has come up with may be able to help her.'

'You've been through a lot, maybe we should wait a while?' I say.

'No, I need to see M now, we're running out of time.'

'Okay,' I say. I can see him getting worked up. 'I'll take you to him.'

Aiden looks like he reconsiders as he realises he'll have to leave Jane.

'I'll stay with her,' Will says, to him. 'I was in the hospital too and I know what she's been through. I'll watch out for her. She'll be okay with me while you're gone.'

Aiden smiles at him. 'Thanks.'

'Okay then,' I say. 'Let's go talk to M. It's time we made contact with the ARC.'

CHAPTER TWENTY-FOUR

I feel a sudden wave of unease as we approach the control tent. It's quieter than usual and I begin to second-guess my decision to talk to M about the cure. Will he think we're crazy? Will he even believe us? All the evidence we have is some symbol drawn on the back of a picture I don't even have anymore.

We enter M's office and find him sitting at his desk, his hands running through his hair as he frowns at his screen.

'M, do you have a moment?' I ask. The few people in the main area of the tent had barely looked at us as we entered, so I have no idea if I've gone about approaching M the right way.

M looks up, dropping his hand from his face. He looks right past me to Aiden, his eyes calculating as he takes in Aiden's dishevelled appearance. He looks like a crazed man so it's not exactly a great impression.

'We need to contact the ARC!' Aiden says, pushing past me to appeal to M. His hands are shaking and there's a desperate plea in his voice that is hard to ignore.

M shakes his head. 'I don't know who you are, but I can tell you now, it's impossible,' he says.

Aiden doesn't let this discourage him. He continues to approach M's desk, walking to one of the chairs and placing his hands down on the back of it. 'Surely you have the means to get in contact?' he says.

'Do you know this guy?' M peers past Aiden to look directly at me.

'M, this is Aiden who worked in West Hope Hospital.'

'Ah,' he replies, his eyes lighting with recognition. He holds out one hand to grasp Aiden's. 'It's great to finally meet you Aiden. I'm glad to see you've been able to join us.'

Aiden ignores the pleasantry. 'We need to get in contact with my grandfather who's in the ARC. He sent a message to me through Elle. He has a cure!'

M doesn't visibly react to the news, but his eyes do narrow on Aiden. 'Who is your grandfather and what ARC?'

'Dr. George Wilson. Aquarius.'

'And you're sure he's figured out a way?'

Aiden glances at me before looking back at M. 'Yes, I'm sure. Can we contact him?'

M pushes his chair from the desk and reclines back in it as he thinks. 'The Government have means to contact their representatives in the ARCs, but that won't do us any good. Our best chance would be to access their network and get a comm through to him. Do you know his username?'

Aiden nods.

'Wait here,' M says. He leaves the two of us in his office and goes down to the main tent next door.

'He changed his tune quickly,' I mutter to Aiden, who nods in agreement. Several minutes later M returns with a man in tow who I recognise.

'This is Gadge,' M says.

'Gadge? You're a part of this?' I ask him.

He looks at me with a blank expression. 'Have we met?' he responds.

I frown. There's absolutely no recognition of me on his face.

'Gadge, it's Elle. I came to your apartment with Hunter and Lara to deal with the tracking on our cuffs. Remember?'

His face still stares at me blankly, not one sign he recognises any of what I've said. I shut my mouth and continue to frown at him.

'I'm sorry, I don't know what you're talking about,' he responds. It doesn't even seem like he's trying to avoid the subject; he looks like he literally can't remember any of it.

I step back and fold my arms across my chest. This is too weird. He really doesn't remember me.

'Gadge's talent enables him to link with electronics. I think he's our best chance at getting into the Aquarius system to contact Dr. Wilson,' M explains.

'It may take me a while, but I think I'm up to the challenge,' Gadge says.

M gives him an approving nod. 'I will set him up on the computer in here, and have him start working on this straight away,' he says. He walks over and clasps Aiden's shoulder. 'You look wrecked. Why don't you get some fresh air while Gadge gets set up?'

Aiden gives an exhausted nod, and I slowly traipse after him as he leaves the tent.

'Are you okay?' I ask, as we slowly follow the path that leads away from camp.

He shrugs and rubs his face tiredly. 'I will be once I've talked to my grandfather.'

'Do you think his cure could help Jane? What will you do if it can't?' I feel selfish asking him this when he's troubled, but I'm also worried about Will and whether the cure can help him too.

His gaze darkens at my comment. 'Then I'll find another way. My grandfather is brilliant and if anyone could find a cure, it's him.' A hint of doubt creeps into his voice and I worry how much he believes the words he's just said.

'She's going to be okay,' I say, though I have no way of knowing if Jane will recover. 'We'll get the cure from your grandfather and it will work.'

He shrugs again. 'We will see.'

We both fall silent as we continue to walk through the forest, each of us anxious about the comm that's about to be put through to the ARC. We both have so much to gain or lose from it.

'We've managed to access their network,' M says, when we return to his office. 'And we've got Dr. Wilson's file and his username up on screen. There's a problem though: his CommuCuff has been removed.'

'Why would they do that?' Aiden asks.

M looks hesitant to answer him. 'He's been put in solitary after attacking one of the nurses in the aged care ward.'

'What?' Aiden says, sinking into one of the chairs by the desk. He looks at me. 'You're the only one here who has seen him recently, do you think he'd do that?'

I chew on my lower lip as I consider my answer. The man had been perfectly fine towards me, but the first time I saw him he was fighting with the nurses who were trying to take him to his testing. 'He did seem to get agitated quickly when he was provoked,' I reply. 'But I'm sure he would never mean to hurt anyone.'

'What do we do?' Aiden asks M.

'Our only chance is if we contact someone on the inside who can get a cuff to him.'

'I know someone who would help,' I say, my heart thundering in my chest. I try not to appear too eager with my suggestion, because if they agree I may just be able to speak to Quinn again.

M considers me, with a questioning look in his eyes.

'I used to live with her and she works in the hospital. She'd be able to get access to him without too many questions being asked.'

'Are you sure she can be trusted?'

'She helped me escape the ARC,' I respond. 'I'd trust her with my life.'

M gives Gadge a nod of approval. 'What's her name?' Gadge asks, as he focuses in on the computer.

'Quinn Roberts.' I can feel tears welling in my eyes as I say her name and take a deep breath to try to control them. My hands are shaking and my heart is hammering in my chest. Am I going to be able to talk with her again?

'Got her file and username,' Gadge says. 'Should I comm her now?'

I look to M, not daring to say anything, but desperately hoping he'll say yes.

'Yes, put in the comm.'

I dash around to stand behind M's desk as the computer display swirls with the electric blue wave that indicates it is connecting.

'Hello?' I stop breathing as I hear Quinn's voice for the first time in months. She sounds confused, which is understandable, because a comm registers who is trying to connect with you. I doubt this comm had a username at all.

'Hello, is anyone there?' she says.

'Quinn?' I whisper.

There is silence on the other end of the comm.

'Quinn, it's Elle,' I say, louder and more certain this time.

'Elle?' Her voice is filled with a sad combination of doubt and hope. The tears that had been welling in my eyes tumble down my cheeks.

'Yes, it's me.'

'Holy shit!' she shouts, through the computer's speaker. She sounds like she's in shock. From her end it must be like getting a comm from a ghost. 'Where the hell are you? Are you okay? How are you comming me? Are you coming back? What's going on?' Her questions are rapidly fired at me in quick succession.

'I can't answer everything now, but I'm fine and so is Sebastian. We're working on a way to get you and everyone out of the ARC.'

'Where are you?' she asks.

I glance up at M who shakes his head at me. 'I can't say.'

'How did you manage to call me? Your CommuCuff has been out of action since you left.'

'We don't have time to explain.'

'We? Who's we? You know I've been worried sick about you right?'

'I've missed you too.'

M gives me a signal to hurry up.

Quinn keeps talking, continuing to fire more questions at me. I'd almost forgotten how eager she can be. 'It's been crazy since you left,' she says. 'So many people have been found tainted and taken away. What's going on? Why's this happening?'

Her questions about the sudden disappearances in the ARC intrigue me, but M waves his hand again to make me hurry. I sigh and try to get back on task. 'Look, Quinn, I actually commed because we need a favour.'

She pauses. 'What do you need?'

'There's a doctor in the aged care ward named Dr. Wilson, you may remember I used to visit him. He has been put in solitary and we need you to get to him with your cuff so we can talk to him.'

'Old man, solitary, cuff, got it,' she says. 'I'm on the other side of the ARC right now, how will you know when I get to the guy?'

I glance at Gadge. 'Quinn,' he says. 'Can you make a comm out on your cuff once you're there? It will register on your file and then we can comm you back.'

'Who's the guy?' she asks. 'He sounds cute.'

I roll my eyes. 'Quinn!' Does she ever think of anything other than cute guys?

'Okay, okay. I'm going now. Elle? I'll get to talk to you again, right?'

I refuse to look at M to see what he says. 'Yes, I'll be here,' I reply.

'Okay, good,' she says. 'Talk soon.' She disconnects the comm before I get a chance to respond.

I take a step back from the desk and close my eyes as I take a deep breath in. I just spoke to Quinn. This isn't a dream.

I feel a hand on my shoulder. 'Why don't you take a seat while we wait?' M asks.

I give him a nod and move to take a seat on the other side of the table, next to Aiden. The room feels incredibly quiet after the conversation with Quinn and I wonder if the others are reeling from it the way I am. They all seem relatively subdued, so I guess making contact with the ARC is as big a deal for them as it is for me.

'You guys were obviously close,' Aiden says, breaking the silence.

'Huh?' I glance at Aiden. 'Sorry, yeah, she's been like a sister to me,' I agree. 'Did you know her?'

He nods. 'Yes, but not very well.' He glances down at his hands, which he is wringing nervously.

'Are you excited to speak to your grandfather again?' I ask.

He continues to focus on his hands. 'Yeah. He could be distant when he was working, but he always made time for me.'

'How do you think he managed to work out the cure? It doesn't sound like he's worked for the hospital for a long time.'

Aiden shakes his head, looking as lost as I am as to the answer. 'I don't know. It doesn't make any sense, but he wouldn't have sent me that message you gave me unless he had. There has to be an explanation.'

'I guess we'll be finding out any minute now,' I say.

We fall back into silence as we wait, the room filling with tension as Gadge and M continue to eye the computer screen for a sign Quinn is ready for the comm. I worry it's taking too long, but continue to remind myself it will probably take a little while for her to get in to see him. As soon as she comms out on her cuff to another user, everyone in the room seems to exhale a breath and Gadge connects us to her.

'Elle?' she says, in answer.

I leap up and walk around the desk to stand behind Gadge. 'Yes, it's me. Are you with him?'

'Yeah,' she says. She sounds uncertain though. 'I don't know what you guys want from him, but I'm not sure if he will be much help.'

'What do you mean?' Aiden says, interrupting.

'He doesn't exactly seem with it,' she says. 'You'll see. Dr. Wilson?' There's the sound of movement in the background. 'Dr. Wilson, I have someone who would like to talk to you.'

'I told you I don't want visitors!' a man yells.

I glance at Aiden, and watch as the colour drains from his face.

'It's not a visitor,' Quinn says. 'It's someone who has commed my cuff to talk to you.'

'No!' Dr. Wilson shouts. 'No visitors. Can't you see I'm busy preparing for the next round of tests.'

'Grandfather?' Aiden says, raising his voice to be heard.

The other end of the comm goes silent.

'Grandfather, it's me, Aiden.'

Still there is no answer.

'Quinn, what's happening?' I ask. 'Is he okay?'

'He's not moving, I think he's in shock,' she says.

'I'm not in shock,' Dr. Wilson mutters. 'Aiden, is that really you?' His voice is louder, like he's closer to the cuff now.

'Yes, it's me. How are you Grandfather?'

'I'd be a whole lot better without these nurses always fluffing about.'

'I'm sure they're just trying to help,' Aiden says.

'Yes, well they're in my way.'

Aiden glances at me. There's worry in his eyes, showing how troubled he is by the way his grandfather is acting.

'Grandfather do you remember sending me a message through a teenage girl named Elle?'

'I did no such thing.'

'Dr. Wilson, this is Elle,' I say. 'You helped me get out of the ARC and gave me a picture of Aiden with a symbol drawn on the back of it to give to him. Do you remember?'

My question is met with silence. Then I swear I can hear sniffling on the other end of the comm. 'Quinn?'

'Are you okay Dr. Wilson?' she asks.

'Leave me alone,' he says.

'Grandfather!' Aiden says, his voice strong and commanding. 'You sent me a message about the cure. What is it? How can I get it?' There's a tinge of desperation to his words. 'Please.'

'Cure? Pah!' Dr Wilson mutters.

'But the message...' Aiden sounds broken as he says this.

'There is no cure,' Dr. Wilson says.

Silent tears run down Aiden's face. 'What's wrong with you? Grandfather?'

'Aiden?' Quinn says. 'I don't think he will say anymore. His eyes are out of focus and he doesn't look like he even knows I'm here.'

'Grandfather?' Aiden says, ignoring what Quinn has said.

I look at M, uncertain what to do, but he doesn't look like he cares about Aiden's grandfather. He looks pissed off. 'Turn the comm off,' M commands Gadge.

'Wait!' I yell, but it's too late as Gadge has already disengaged the comm.

'You didn't let us say goodbye!' I accuse.

'There is no cure, I will not waste another second on this folly. You can both go now,' M says.

'You don't know that! He must know about a cure,' I say.

'I will not waste another moment of our resources on a raving old man. Leave!'

I grab Aiden's arm and pull him from the office. He looks shocked and it's not until we're outside again that he even seems to recognise where we are.

'Elle?' he says, as we leave the tent. 'Even if my grandfather had a cure, he's in no state to remember and there's no way for us to get in contact with him again. We have no cure and time is running out. I think Jane is going to die...'

CHAPTER TWENTY-FIVE

I try not to let Aiden's words upset me, but they resonate in my mind. 'Jane is going to die.' I don't even know the girl, but I feel such a connection to her and it could easily be me in her position right now.

Aiden refuses to leave the clinic again once he returns to Jane's side. Between him and the other doctors, they work around the clock trying to find a way to fix her. But days pass by without any change in her stats and I can see her lack of recovery is slowly destroying him. Sometimes she seems close to consciousness, as she mumbles in her sleep, but she's yet to wake up, and I worry she never will.

I commit myself to the tests the doctors here put me through, hoping desperately it will help. I only wish there was more I could do as there's been little change to Will's health either.

April doesn't come back to camp for days, so when she finally returns she can't wait to have me back training to use my talents again. As I head towards the hanger to meet her I notice Gadge standing in the shadow of one of the trees watching me.

'Gadge?' I ask, slowly approaching him.

He shies away and takes several steps back, allowing the shadow to further cloak him. Again, I get the feeling he doesn't recognise me, which is strange. I only just saw him the other day.

'Gadge, it's me, Elle, from the other day,' I say, softly.

He looks down at the ground and fidgets restlessly, refusing to look at me.

'Is everything okay?' I ask him. I look around to see if there's anyone else about who can help me get him back to camp, but we're completely alone.

He opens his mouth as though to speak, but then shuts it again. He seems confused and scared. His eyes are wide and his breathing is laboured.

I crouch down on the ground and look up at him. 'Hey, it's okay. Why don't we get you back to camp with the others?'

'Not-t s-safe,' he stutters. I glance over my shoulder, but the woods behind me are empty.

'What do you mean?'

'Not-t s-safe,' he repeats. His eyes latch onto mine and I can see his fear clearly behind the look he's giving me. He reaches out and wraps his hand tightly around my CommuCuff. 'F-find him,' he says, before abruptly letting go and running away from me, becoming lost in the woods moments later.

'Gadge?' I call after him, but silence meets my words. He's gone.

I slowly stand and as I do I look down at my cuff to see a name written across the screen. Henry Moore. I look up at the area of forest where Gadge disappeared. What could I possibly need with Henry Moore?

APRIL IS ALREADY SEATED on the ground in the centre of the hangar when I get there, her legs are crossed and her eyes shut. She looks peaceful and I push down an irrational surge of envy. I will never be able to maintain such composure without my inhibitor band on.

'The strangest thing just happened,' I say, as I take a seat on the ground across from her.

Her eyes blink open and settle on me. 'Hey yourself,' she says. 'What happened?'

I shake my head. 'It doesn't matter,' I reply, feeling spooked by Gadge's behaviour and not wanting to relive it. 'Could you help me find someone?'

'Who?'

'A guy named Henry Moore. Does the name ring a bell?'

She shrugs. 'I haven't heard of him before, but I can check him out. What do you need to know?'

'If you could just find out where he lives...' I answer.

She frowns as she watches me. 'Have you tried asking M about this?'

I pause as I consider how to respond to her question. I don't know why Gadge was scared, but what if he was scared of M? Until I know who Henry Moore is, it's probably best not to involve him. Part of me doesn't even want to tell April about it, but I don't have any choice if I want a realistic chance of finding him.

'I'm not sure if I trust him, and to be honest, I doubt he'll even listen to me right now.' I don't like admitting my distrust for him to April, but I need to be open with her. He was quick to lie to us about not being able to contact the ARC when he clearly could. I worry about what else he might be keeping from us.

April raises one eyebrow and folds her arms across her chest. 'You can trust him. He can sometimes be a bit tough, but it's only because he's looking out for the well-being of everyone as a whole.'

'Can we just keep him out of this for the moment?' I plead. 'Surely you can look into where he is without raising any flags?'

April hesitates, and looks like she's going to continue to fight me on this, but then sighs. 'Fine. You're probably right about him not listening to you right now, I heard about the mess with Dr. Wilson. I'll have a snoop and see what I can dig up. Should we get started with your training?'

I nod and proceed to remove the band.

LATER THAT NIGHT, April comes by my tent. Kelsey is in a deep sleep, but I've been tossing and turning for hours.

She shakes my arm gently to wake me. 'Can we talk outside?' she whispers.

I glance at Kelsey and nod, following her out of the tent.

'How did you get the name Henry Moore?' she asks, once we're outside.

I shake my head. 'It doesn't matter.'

'Elle, where did you get the name?'

I consider telling her the truth, but something stops me. Gadge had been acting strangely when he gave it to me, and if she knew the truth she may not look into the man's whereabouts. It seemed important to Gadge I find him.

'I think I heard his name in the hospital,' I lie. 'Why? Did you find anything on him?'

She sighs and nods. 'It's not good.'

'What do you mean, it's not good?'

She glances over her shoulder into the darkness of the trees behind her before facing me again. 'He didn't come up on the reintegration system. So, I checked the ARC systems, and he wasn't there either, which is strange. There are always records of people on at least the ARC system. I checked again, going deeper this time. His file was encrypted, but we found it.'

'Who is he?'

'He was a lead scientist in the Aries ARC, but now he's being held at the government headquarters.'

'Why?'

'Because they think he can create a cure.'

I take a step back from her. 'What?'

She shakes her head. 'I don't know how you heard of this guy, but he's important and M will do anything to have him here with us.'

'So, M knows?'

She looks away from me. 'Yeah, he knows. There was no way I'd be able to get that level of access without his resources. I had to tell him. '

I nod, feeling slightly betrayed she was so quick to tell M, but also understanding it had to be done. 'So, if this guy can do what you say he can, we're getting him out, right?'

She digs her hands into her pockets and huffs out a breath. 'That's the last place I'd want to break someone out of, but we're going to have to. He could prove vital to everything we're trying to achieve.'

'When can we do it?'

'I'll need a few days to organise the extraction team, but you won't be coming anywhere.'

'You can't expect me to stay here while you guys go.'

'Actually, I can,' she says. 'You have barely any control over your talents. You'd be a liability. I won't put other people in danger because you want to tag along. Not to mention the fact they have an alert out for you. You'd be walking right to them, which is exactly what they want. Look, I'll keep you in the loop with what's happening, but that's all I can do.'

'I don't need to be talented to be useful,' I say.

April shakes her head. 'For this, you do. I have to head back to the Mason's tonight, but I'll be back tomorrow. We can do a training session then and I'll let you know how I'm getting on with the preparations.'

She looks at me closely, waiting for a response, but I refuse to meet her eyes. She huffs out a short breath when I don't say anything. 'I'll see you in the morning,' she says, turning to walk away. I watch her disappear between the trees.

Once she's gone I don't return to my bed. Instead, I stroll away from the tents and out of the woods to the open concrete expanse. When I get far enough away from everything I sit and close my eyes.

I take deep breaths, trying to ground myself.

'I'm not a liability,' I murmur. With that I open my eyes and take my inhibitor band off my wrist, placing it beside me. I feel the rush of my talents being freed. I've slowly become accustomed to it in my sessions with April. But, without her here to help control my confidence, my fears easily resurface and they feel stronger and more erratic than I'm used to.

My fingers tingle and I try to ignore the sensation and focus on my sense of smell, like April had taught me. It helps a little, but not enough. My fingers itch to move, and I can feel power surging through my body and down my arms to my fingertips.

The feeling unnerves me, which only makes it stronger.

'You can do this Elle,' I tell myself aloud. I take a deep breath in through my nose and blow it out through my mouth. My heart only beats faster, and I can feel drops of sweat building on the back of my neck.

I clench my hands into fists and place them down on the ground beside me. Doing so makes the rest of my body tingle and the hair on my head slowly lifts of its own accord, as though it's alive with static electricity.

I squint my eyes shut again. 'Concentrate Elle.'

I'm rattled though and the erratic energy pulsing through me is only getting stronger. I try to concentrate on each sense, like I would with April, but I'm overwhelmed by the power inside of me.

I clench my teeth together and I hold my body tense. I just want it out of me. I want it gone. I groan as my body shakes with it.

I need it out of me. I can't take it anymore. 'Just go!' I scream. My whole body sags as the energy rushes out of me. It's as though the floodgates have been opened and my talent has flowed out of me in one intense outburst.

As I slowly open my eyes I gasp. The dirt and pebbles that were on the ground around me are now floating through the air with tiny bolts of electricity dancing between them. I scramble to my feet and reach my hand out to grasp one of the small stones that floats leisurely by me, like it were an airborne feather. The tiny sparks that radiate along its surface transfer onto the back of my hand. They feel like a pencil lightly drawing on me as they skim across the top of my skin. Slowly each tiny bolt extinguishes into nothing.

When I look around me, I feel as though I've stepped into a sandstorm, that's been frozen for a moment in time, with a thousand tiny thunderbolts flashing between the small grains of sand. It's magical the way they flicker and crackle, and it's like I'm inside a spitting sparkler, illuminating the night around me.

I didn't want to use my talents when I took the inhibitor off. All I wanted was to prove I could sit there and control them enough to have nothing happen. I couldn't even slightly do that.

'Elle?' A voice yells, beyond my pocket of electric dust. I can't see anyone, as they are hidden behind the wall of dirt I've surrounded myself in, but I'd know Sebastian's voice anywhere.

The dirt and electricity all plunges to the ground in one heavy drop and I see him running across the open plain towards me. I kneel down and pick up the inhibitor, placing it back on my wrist.

April was right. Without her, I have no control over these talents of mine whatsoever. I am a burden.

'Are you okay?' he shouts, when he gets closer.

'I'm fine.'

'I heard you scream.'

'How? I didn't think anyone would be able to hear me out here.'

He stops and leans on his knees as he catches his breath for a moment. He looks a little guilty. 'I couldn't help but overhear your conversation with April earlier. When you didn't come back to your tent, I came looking to check you were alright.'

'You heard that?'

'Yes.'

I wrap my arms around my body and try to avoid looking at him directly in his eyes. 'I wish you hadn't.'

'Why?'

'I don't want you to think I'm a liability.'

'Are you serious?' he asks. 'You are the last person I'd think was a liability. April doesn't give you credit for the things you've achieved, all of which you did without having talents yourself.'

I shrug. 'She's right though, I can't control myself.'

'Control will come, but you were right, you have as much right to be a part of the team as anyone.'

I sigh. 'Not if people could get hurt because they're trying to look out for me.'

'Look, leave April to me. You should be there.'

'Maybe I shouldn't, I just proved her right. I shouldn't be going anywhere. I'll only put others in danger. If me not going means a better chance of getting the cure, I have to accept that.'

'Elle, you can't doubt yourself. It only makes controlling your talent harder.'

I kick at one of the rocks by my feet. 'I think we all need to come to terms with the fact that maybe some talents can't be controlled and mine is one of them.'

'Don't give up on yourself yet,' he says. 'You may surprise everyone still.'

He looks at me, seeming confident I'll overcome this. I wish more than anything I could be the girl he sees in me, but I feel like I'm failing.

'I hope so,' I reply, though I can feel my doubts swelling inside.

CHAPTER TWENTY-SIX

'Still no change?' I ask Aiden, as I enter the medical clinic and approach Jane's bed. I pass him the sandwich I brought for him from the mess tent and pull up a chair to sit next to him.

'Thanks,' he croaks, taking it from me. 'And no, no change.' His eyes hold such terror as he watches her. I worry how he'll go on if she doesn't make it.

'I'm sorry we didn't wait for you the night we escaped,' I say.

'I'm glad you didn't,' he replies. 'We all could have been caught if you'd waited any longer. April made the right call.'

We can't know for sure what would have happened if we'd stayed, but it comforts me to know he believes it was the right decision. 'Why did you both stay there for so long?'

'I was a part of a small team working on a way to stop the accelerated mutations that affected people who surfaced too soon when I met Jane. The mutations were slowly killing her and we both agreed her best chance of survival was in the hospital where I could help. I guess we were both wrong.'

His face screws up and I can easily see how much it torments him that he made the wrong decision. It's not his fault and he didn't do this to her, but he doesn't see it that way.

'Has there been any luck with the blood samples the doctors took from me?' I ask, attempting to change the subject.

He shakes his head. 'No. I've spent years working on a cure and made little progress. Even with your blood samples, we're still a long way off.'

My shoulders sag and I look away from him. I worry about how long it will take them to find a way to help Will and Jane. A part of me thought they'd take one look at my blood and come up with an answer, but that's clearly not the case.

'I haven't given up hope yet, and you shouldn't either,' he says.

I glance over my shoulder to Will, who is still asleep at the other end of the room, before looking back at Aiden. 'How is Will really doing?' I ask, keeping my voice low.

'It's hard to say. He seems to be steadily declining. If we don't figure something out to help him soon, I fear the worst for him.'

I swallow uncomfortably. I want to turn and look at the sleeping boy again, but I can't bring myself to do it. I can't stand the thought of losing him.

'He's a fighter. He will be okay,' I say, more to comfort myself than anything else. 'I stumbled upon a spot in the forest yesterday that has all these amazing flowers. I'm planning to surprise him with it once he's a bit better. He misses the outside.'

'I'm sure he'll love that,' Aiden replies, though I catch a concerned look in his eyes.

I hear movement behind me, and turn to find Sebastian walking in.

'Elle, I'm glad I found you,' he says, pulling one hand through his hair. 'April is back and she needs to talk with you.'

'She's back already?' Sebastian nods. 'Okay, I'm coming now. Can I get you anything while I'm out?' I ask Aiden.

'No, I'm fine.'

'I haven't seen you eat anything in days. You should eat.' I nod my head at the sandwich he holds limply in his hands.

'Yes, Mum,' he replies, but the humour fails to reach his eyes. I don't think he'll give the sandwich a second look once I'm gone, but I can hardly stand over him to watch him eat it.

'Okay, I'll see you later,' I say, before following Sebastian outside. Every time I leave Aiden in the clinic I feel bad. The thought of him there, spending all day and all night desperately struggling to find a cure for Jane is heartbreaking. I just wish I could do more to help.

I allow Sebastian to lead the way as we walk over to April's tent. She's at the Mason's almost every night and barely uses it, so I haven't been there before. She ushers us inside as soon as we arrive.

'I need a window maker for getting to Henry,' she says, as soon as she zips the front flap shut. 'Dalton is stationed in North Hope for M at the moment and he's the only one we have.'

'If you need someone to get to the other side of a wall, surely you could ask Ryan to help?' I suggest.

She shakes her head. 'Ryan is doing stuff for M, he won't be able to help us with this.'

'I could do it,' Sebastian says.

She shakes her head again. 'No, your talent won't help as there's more than one person involved.' She looks at me seriously.

'What?' I ask her, when she fails to explain.

'I want you to be the window maker,' she says.

'Is this a joke?' I ask, thoroughly unimpressed.

'Do you think I'd joke about something like this?'

'No, but it's crazy. I don't think I even have that talent,' I say.

This hardly dissuades her. 'The doctors here have samples from everyone in camp. They could give you the talent.'

'Can't Dalton come back and help?'

April shakes her head. 'He'd raise suspicion if he left at the moment. It needs to be you.'

'I thought you said it would be too dangerous for Elle to go there because of the alert the recruiters have out for her?' Sebastian says.

'We should be able to get by them without any trouble. I'll convince anyone who sees her that she's someone else.'

'Don't you think Elle has enough talents to deal with already?' Sebastian adds.

April ignores him. 'I've only been giving you a bit of help with keeping your emotions in check during our training sessions. I can do a lot more than that. I could have you convinced you are Dalton if that helps, but it's the best chance we have.'

I glance at Sebastian, who looks as unimpressed with April's suggestion as I feel. Maybe with her help I could do it. My hopes sink though as I think of Ryan's warning. He made me promise not to take on any other talents, but could one more really hurt? How can I say no, when without Henry there would be no cure for Will and Jane?

'Okay, I'll do it. But don't make me think I'm Dalton, I'll lose half my vocabulary.'

April laughs. 'I think that should be fine.'

I suddenly feel nervous about the idea, but I try to hide how I feel. What if I already have too much to handle? What if gaining a new talent changes me too much?

'When will we do it?' I say, pushing my concerns aside.

'I think we should get them to dose you with the talent now, so you can practice using it before we go in for Henry tomorrow.'

'You want to go tomorrow?' I ask, struggling to keep the alarm from my voice. I don't even know how long it takes for a talent to take effect once I've been dosed with it. What if it takes a week?

She nods. 'There's a celebration in the city to commemorate the day it was founded tomorrow. It should make it easier for us to get in and out of Headquarters. I've already got the other member of our team organised.'

'Who else is coming?'

'Soren.'

'And me,' Sebastian adds.

'No, you're not coming,' April responds, without missing a beat.

'To hell I'm not. You can't send Elle in there and expect me to wait at home like a good boy. You know I can help.'

April watches him as she thinks it through. 'You can come with us to Headquarters, but you're not coming inside.'

'No, I'm coming inside.'

'Look, if you come inside there will be too many of us and we'll be caught. You can come, but you need to wait outside in case something goes wrong. It's the only way I'll let you come.'

He glances at me uneasily. 'Fine,' he agrees.

'Come on, let's get you to the clinic, so we can get you your new talent,' April says. She sounds way too chirpy about the idea, which I find odd and slightly concerning. Last night I wasn't allowed to come at all.

When the doctor brings out the syringe he intends to use on me, I nearly turn and walk out of the clinic. The thing is huge, and reminds me so much of the one they'd used during my eye treatment in the hospital. The serum inside even has an equally unnatural shade of purple to it. The sight of it shakes me, but despite my reservations, I lie down on the bed opposite Will's.

Sebastian pulls up a chair and takes hold of one of my hands. 'You've got this,' he says, with a grin.

I grumble, but nod anyway, refusing to look away from his bright blue eyes as the doctor proceeds to place the needle in the crook of my other arm. The injection is slow and painful. I clench my teeth together to stop myself from screaming out and squeeze Sebastian's hand so tightly I'm probably close to breaking it.

He prattles away to me about nothing, but at least he somewhat distracts me while the pain passes.

'How long will it take to be effective?' April asks the doctor, once he's finished with my injection.

'We've never done this before, so there's no way to be sure.'

'Should we go to the hangar to see if it's working?' she asks me.

I nod and try to push myself up, but the motion makes me light-headed. I feel sweaty and weaker than I had felt moments before.

Not to mention a little bit queasy ... I quickly clamber to the side of the bed and throw up in the bin next to it.

'Are you okay?' Sebastian asks, rushing to my side.

'Sure,' I reply, trying to sound better than I feel. He offers me a tissue box and I quickly grab one and try to subtly wipe my mouth with it. I cringe, unable to believe I was just sick in front of everyone.

'Maybe we should keep you for observation for a while,' the doctor says.

I nod gratefully and lie back on the bed. I'd forgotten how sick the treatments in the hospital had made me feel. If this is what it feels like to gain a talent, I'll be glad if I can manage to stop it.

It's several hours before I feel even slightly normal again. Will is having a good day, so he offers me a distraction by introducing me to one of the lab rats. I don't think I've ever seen him so excited before. He's even given them all names, including one called Elle. I'm not too sure how I feel about a rat being named after me, but it seems to make him happy and, in a way, I guess it's kind of sweet.

When April comes back to check on me, I'm feeling much better and the doctor agrees I should be okay to go. We head out to the hangar where we've been doing all my training. Much to April's annoyance, Sebastian follows us there. It's like he doesn't want to let me out of his sight and I don't know whether to be grateful or worried.

Instead of sitting in the centre of the building like we usually would, April leads me over to one of the walls. I remove the inhibitor band from my wrist and place it on the floor.

'How do you feel?' April asks.

I think about it for a moment. 'I feel good,' I respond, smiling. 'Really good.' I look at the wall and I can actually picture making a window in it, just like Dalton would. It doesn't seem like simply a possibility. It's something I *know* I can do.

April must be manipulating me to the max to make me feel so sure of myself. I'm vaguely aware I shouldn't feel this way, but I find it doesn't bother me. Who wouldn't want to be this calm and confident?

She gives me a nod. 'Do you want to make a window?'

I grin. Hell yeah I do. I place one hand firmly against the cold metal wall, and with my other hand I slowly draw a large circle with one finger around the outside. I focus on the wild, pent-up forces inside of me and will the energy to move down my arm, through my hand and into my forefinger. I can feel the shift inside of me as I do this, and my finger begins to throb and throw off tiny sparks, which build until my finger is glowing a strange shade of blue-tinged white light.

A glowing trail follows my finger. It feels connected to me, and I can sense every element of it as though it were a cord extending from my finger. Once the circle is complete, I channel the energy inside of me into my other hand, which slowly starts to radiant pure, bright light. I imagine the wall inside the circle is like a series of millions and millions of tiny particles and I urge them all to disperse.

They slowly trickle away, like tiny seeds of a dandelion head disappearing as they are scattered in the wind. The hole is slow to form at first, but before I know it, I can clearly see the sun beaming down on the hard concrete ground on the other side of the window.

A wisp of wind catches a strand of my hair, blowing it across my face from through the window and I smile. The process felt natural and as easy as taking a deep breath in and out. I almost feel sad as I remove my hand from the wall and the window disappears. I face April and Sebastian, beaming. 'How was that?'

April claps her hands together. 'That was incredible!' She bends down to collect my inhibitor and passes it to me. For the first time in forever I feel whole, like I'm not out of control or bottling up a part of me that wants to escape. For once I don't want to put the inhibitor back on.

I slowly place it back around my wrist. I feel a wave of sadness as my talents are clamped back inside me. They had just filled me with such joy and now it's like they are locked away in a box where I can't access them.

'You did really well,' April says. 'You'll be brilliant tomorrow.'

'Are you sure you're not rushing into this?' Sebastian asks her.

'I've run the logistics and tomorrow is our best bet.' She glances down at her cuff. 'I have dinner with the Masons so I should run. But, I'll meet you both here tomorrow afternoon at two o'clock.'

She races off and I am left alone with Sebastian.

'Do you think this is being rushed into?' I ask him.

'I'm not sure,' he replies. 'It does feel like it's happening very quickly. You're still as white as a sheet after that injection, are you sure you're feeling up to this?'

'Yes, I feel okay now. Besides, I don't have any choice but to be okay. They need my help and I want to give it in any way I can.'

He frowns, unhappy with my answer. 'I just hope we don't run into any trouble tomorrow.'

'Me too,' I agree.

CHAPTER TWENTY-SEVEN

The next morning moves by in a blur of nerves and anxiety. Every time I think about using my talents and the people relying on them, my heart flutters and my palms grow sweaty.

I still remember how amazing it felt when April helped me take control of them but, without her influence, doubts easily creep back in. I worry something will go wrong and I'll lose control.

I'm silent as I walk with Sebastian over to the hangar I've been training in. My fingers tap anxiously against my thighs and I chew on my lower lip as I try to avoid thinking of what we're about to do.

'It's going to be fine,' Sebastian says, when he catches a look at me.

'And what if it's not?' I reply.

'It will be. We both know what an obsessive control freak April can be. Usually, it's annoying as hell, but it also means she's been meticulous in planning this out. This will work.'

'I suppose,' I mumble, not completely convinced.

He stops walking and takes both my hands in his. 'I won't ever let anything bad happen to you ever again.'

'Some things can't be stopped,' I reply, staring intently at his chest.

With one hand he gently lifts my chin so I look him in the eyes. The colour is such a deep shade of blue in the afternoon light, like the dark depths of the sea, swirling with emotion. He looks troubled, but there's also a hint of passion that traps me in his stare. When he looks at me this way I struggle to remember to breathe.

'I promise I will protect you,' he says.

'Even from myself?' I say, with a sad laugh.

'Even from yourself.'

'Are you two coming?' April shouts at us from the hangar, causing us to jump apart like we've just been caught doing something wrong.

'Just a sec!' Sebastian calls back.

We start moving to the hangar again. I have to stop myself from reaching out to Sebastian. I just want him close to me, even if we were only holding hands. I clench my hands into fists and try to stop myself from having those ideas. They're exactly why I've distanced myself from him. I need to focus. Especially today.

'I don't think you'll need my help though,' Sebastian says, continuing our conversation. 'You seem to have that covered already.'

I smile. 'Well, the band does,' I say, nodding at the inhibitor.

'You give that thing too much power over you. If you could just believe in yourself, I doubt you'd need it at all.' He seems sad about my reliance on the device. I don't like it either, but I don't have any other choice.

Soren is already at the hangar when we get there and April seems restless as she waits for our arrival. 'Let's go,' she says, as soon as we reach them. 'I'll explain everything on the way.'

We follow her as she leads us across the expanse of concrete towards the city that lies ahead. I feel nervous and excited as we walk. It feels like forever since I've been in the city and I find I actually miss it.

'Where is Headquarters?' I ask April, as we reach the marsh that divides the camp from the city.

'It's in East Hope, near the Reintegration Centre. It's this ugly old building that looks like it would crumble if a strong enough storm hit it.'

'And that's where they chose their HQ to be?'

She shrugs. 'I wouldn't have picked it.'

'How are we getting inside?'

'Let me worry about that. Just remember, you are the window maker today, that's all I want you to concern yourself with.'

I nod and try to appear confident, but the mention of using my talent causes my stomach to drop. What if I can't do it again? Or worse, what if I end up exploding like I did in the hospital and I hurt someone?

'Oh, here, put this on,' April says, passing me a hoodie from out of her backpack.

'What's this for?' I ask.

'To try and cover up your appearance a bit. I can still manipulate any recruiters that recognise you, but it will be better if they don't. Try to keep the hood up and your head down if we see anyone.'

It doesn't take long for us to make it to the more populated part of the city. I see signs of people and occupied buildings more quickly than I expected. I remember it taking such a long time the night we escaped. But, I was carrying Kelsey and dead on my feet, so it's not surprising it took longer.

There's a bright, happy air to the place as we move onto some of the busier streets. People appear excited and many of them are waving purple pieces of material. There seems to be purple banners everywhere. There are celebrations going on inside the cafes and restaurants we pass. It's as though the whole city has gone on holiday and I feel completely out of place.

'Do they do this every year?' I ask April.

'Yep, it seems to get bigger with each one. I've never seen so much purple in the streets before.'

Soren grimaces, as he looks at all the purple surrounding us. The look on his face is of such disgust it makes me want to laugh, but after seeing what he can do to people, I wouldn't dare.

Sebastian lightly touches my arm and I hang back from the others to talk with him. 'Are you alright?' he asks.

I glance at April and Soren who are walking several feet in front of us. 'Am I that obvious?'

'No, not at all. I just happen to know when you twist your hands that way, there's usually something up.'

'Oh.' I instantly drop my hands to my sides and we slowly follow them again. 'I'm nervous about using my talent again. I'm not sure if I'm ready.'

'You were brilliant yesterday.'

'No, April was brilliant. Without her I'm like a ticking time bomb, just waiting to go off. What if something goes wrong while we're in there?'

'It won't,' he says.

'But what if it does?'

He folds his arms across his chest. 'You shouldn't worry. If something goes wrong, you comm me and I'll come and get you.'

'Can you teleport into a place you haven't been before?'

'Not easily. But once I'm in I can get you out.'

I sigh and rub my face with my hands. 'That doesn't sound like much of a back up plan.'

'It's better than nothing.'

'I suppose,' I reply.

'We're nearly there,' April calls to us, over her shoulder.

Sebastian grabs my hand and squeezes it tightly. 'Everything will be fine. Don't lose sight of why we're doing this.'

'You're right,' I say, smiling up at him. 'We'll be able to help Jane and Will.'

April leads us to the entrance of a towering apartment building. She walks confidently through the front doors and straight towards one of the elevators inside. The place reminds me a lot of the Mason's. The outside looks like a shard of glass reaching to poke a hole in the sky and inside the floor is covered in marble tiles with white walls and shiny steel fixtures.

We go to an apartment on the eighteenth floor, which is gutted inside, with bland concrete floors and walls and electrical wires hanging from the ceiling. It's not nearly as impressive as the building that holds it.

April picks up a bag just inside the front door and passes us each a black uniform from inside. 'You need to change here; we're just around the corner from Headquarters now.'

I hold out the black recruiter's uniform she's passed me and push down a wave of unease. Without the hood I'm wearing now, anyone could spot me.

'You should probably wear this too,' April says, passing me a ball of blonde hair.

'You think a wig will work?' I ask, holding it up.

She shrugs. 'It'll help.'

We each go to a separate room in the apartment to change. It feels wrong putting the black suit on. Something about it just makes me edgy. Once I have the wig on I walk back to join the others.

Sebastian bursts out laughing when he sees the wig.

'Well, that just makes me feel great,' I grumble.

He comes and pats me on the top of the head. 'No, I think it's cute,' he says, grinning broadly. 'But I definitely prefer brunettes,' he whispers, in my ear.

April hands us each an ID badge, then motions us in the direction of the door. 'We should go,' she announces, causing the smile to drop from my face. My heart leaps into my mouth and as I take one last look at the empty apartment I feel a flood of uncertainty wash through me. I'm not ready for this. I'm not ready for this at all.

CHAPTER TWENTY-EIGHT

I feel like a thousand eyes are watching me as we approach the headquarters building. My skin tingles with anxiety and I keep my eyes focused down on the ground before me as I try to fit in. But with my black recruiter's clothes, I doubt there's any chance of that happening.

The old stone building stands behind a large square, which features a fountain in its centre. There are people everywhere waving their bright purple banners, music fills the air and the place buzzes with excitement. We leave Sebastian at the edge of the crowd, where he has a good view of the building.

'Be safe,' he whispers to me, drawing me in for a hug before I leave.

'You too,' I respond. 'Don't do anything stupid.'

'What, like escaping the ARC to go after my friend? I wouldn't dream of it.' He grins.

I groan and take a step away, ignoring his comment, which only makes him laugh. 'I'll see you in a bit,' I tell him.

As we move through the crowd April falls into step next to me. 'Stay close to me and do everything I do once we're inside. They'll have cameras in there, monitoring our every movement. We need to blend in if we don't want to be discovered,' she says, keeping her voice low.

I don't respond and she raises one eyebrow as she looks to me, checking to see I've heard her. I give her a cursory nod in response.

As we near the entrance, I notice hideous stone gargoyles, watching us from their perches on the roof of the building. The monsters give me the creeps and I try to ignore them as we move closer. My eyes drop to the recruiters manning the entrance, which only makes my nerves worse. They stand there with blank stares as they watch the square in front of them, but to me they're more terrifying than the gruesome stone creatures above.

April and I enter Headquarters first, with Soren waiting to enter a few minutes after us. The inside of the building is a whole lot more modern than the outside. Black marble tiles cover the floor and several cool, steel elevator doors line the wall opposite the entrance. There's a desk in the corner, which a tall woman in a recruiter's uniform stands behind. A row of turnstiles that stretches from one end of the room to the other bars our way to the lifts.

April moves up to one and scans her ID badge against the sensor. I walk to the one next to her to do the same. Hers beeps happily, allowing her entrance. I move against the bar to walk forward too, but the bar doesn't budge.

I scan the ID again, but three successive, angry beeps sound in response. I can feel adrenaline starting to pulse through my system as I push the ID badge against the scanner again.

Beep, beep, beep. I'm denied entry again.

I look up to April, to see what I should do, but she's walking towards the lift, completely oblivious to what's going on. A part of me worries this is a part of her plan, but mostly I worry about what I'll do next.

'Are you having problems?' the woman behind the desk calls to me.

I look at her and nod. She waves me over to the desk and I take slow steps towards her. Each one feels heavy and my heart beats faster the closer and closer I get. What will she do with me if I'm found out?

Would I go back to the hospital? They can't know who I really am.

She holds her hand out for my ID badge, which I pass to her. She takes the badge and presses it against the scanner on her desk. Each second she holds it there, I get closer to making a run for it.

How quickly could she pursue me? Would Sebastian see me trying to escape and help?

Before I make a move the woman passes the badge back to me.

'That's fine Abby, you can head on through,' she says, pointing to the gate next to her. 'Sorry for the delay, that turnstile has been playing up for weeks. Don't know when they're planning to send someone to fix it.'

'Thanks,' I reply, moving through the gate, my sweaty hand grasping the badge as tightly as it can. April has just entered one of the lifts and I race to catch up with her.

'Hold the lift,' I call out to her, making it through the doors just in time before they close.

'What was the hold up?' April asks.

'Badge wouldn't scan, apparently the turnstile I went to is broken.'

She nods and taps her badge against the scanner in the lift, before pressing the button for level -10, lighting it up. I feel my stomach drop as we plummet quickly down below the ground.

'Where is Soren?' I ask.

'He's going to access security.'

'He's not coming with us?' Surely we need his help.

'No, we'll be fine without him. Sub-level 10 isn't high security.'

I look at the numbers lighting up as we pass each floor. 'Why isn't Henry Moore in the hospital?' I mumble, as we go past level -6.

'From what I can gather, they're making sure he doesn't give anyone the cure, rather than having him do the research. Maybe he refused,' April replies.

The lift doors open and we're met with a room filled with pitch-black darkness. We step out of the lift and a light flickers on to reveal a long corridor, lined by glass walls. As we move away from the lift, I get a better look at them and can see each thick pane of glass holds a cell behind it. There is no visible door to get in or out.

The first few cells are empty, but then we come across ones with occupants inside. Most prisoners are cowering in the corner of their rooms, not daring to look up at the people who have entered and returned the light to their darkened world.

'What did these people do to deserve being imprisoned like this?' I ask April.

She shrugs. 'They obviously pissed someone off.'

'Can't we help them?'

April sighs sadly and shakes her head. 'One day we will, but for now Henry is the only one we can help.'

I watch the poor prisoners as we move past each cell, with total sympathy. The sight of them disturbs me to my core. No one deserves to be locked up this way and living in the dark. It's even worse than the hospital and I wouldn't wish that upon anyone.

April stops by one of the cells and motions me closer. 'It's empty,' she says, and then swears. 'He was supposed to be in here!' she practically growls.

'What do we do?'

'We wait until Soren can access security and we'll see if he can find him from there.'

She starts to move back towards the lift. I go to follow her, but stop as my eyes land on a long dark mop of hair behind one of the glass walls. My heart stops beating for a brief second before I launch myself against the glass.

'April! Lara's in there!'

Inside the glass cell I can see Lara, huddled in a ball in the corner, her hair knotted and draping down over her face. I place my hand against the glass, hoping she'll look up to see we're here, but she sinks further back into the corner.

'Is she okay?' I ask April.

'We're about to find out. Take your inhibitor off!' April replies.

I nod and frantically take it off, anxious to get Lara out of this hell. I barely notice the rush I feel as my talents are released, my focus is completely upon Lara and my horror at what they've done to her. With one finger I trace a large circle in the glass, making a window, just like I did yesterday. The glass disappears and April steps through, into the cell.

'Lara?' she says. Lara doesn't respond, so she crouches down beside her. 'It's Beth and Elle, from school.' The sound of our names makes her go still. Ever so slowly she peers up at April.

'Beth?' she asks, her eyes welling with tears. She glances at me and quickly lowers her eyes, pulling back further, which makes my heart drop. She must blame me for this. Of course she does. I'm the reason she went to the Reintegration Centre and she wouldn't be here if it wasn't for me.

'Elle's wearing a blonde wig,' April explains.

I'd completely forgotten. No wonder she shied away. I pull the wig from my head. 'Hey Lara,' I say. 'You should be able to feel it's me, right?'

She shakes her head and lifts her arm to reveal a device on her wrist just like my inhibitor band. 'I couldn't even if I tried, not with this,' she says. Her voice is frail and croaks as she talks.

'It's okay, we can worry about the band later,' April says, gently easing her arm under Lara to try and help her stand. 'C'mon, we're getting you out of here.'

Tears start rolling down Lara's cheeks as April helps her stand. 'Is this happening?' she says, as they stagger towards me.

April nods. 'Yes, now don't worry about talking, we don't want to tire you out.'

The two of them move out of the cell and I lift my hand off the glass, closing the window, once they have passed through.

'You can put your band back on now,' April says.

I quickly jam it back on my wrist and go to the other side of Lara to help April support her as we walk.

We are nearly to the lift when Lara stops walking. 'We can't leave,' she says, her eyes going wide with fear.

'What's wrong?' April asks.

'They have my father. We can't leave without him.'

'We don't have a choice,' April says. 'We can't rescue him too.'

'No!' she yells, taking a step back, her eyes going wild and her body shaking. 'We have to get him.'

I look at April pleadingly. 'Surely we can get him too?' I ask, before turning to Lara. 'Who's your father? Where is he?'

'His name is Henry,' she sobs. 'They have him in a lab somewhere.'

We both freeze as her words descend on us. 'Are you talking about Henry Moore?' I ask.

She nods. 'Yes, that's him. I have my mum's name, Taylor.'

'Henry is your father?' April asks, barely registering as Lara continues to nod. April doesn't miss a beat and her cuff is already up at her lips, while I still stare at Lara, dumbfounded.

'Soren are you there?' April asks.

Lara crumbles to the ground and starts shaking. I rush over and start rubbing her back, in an effort to comfort her. What have the monsters here done to her? The spunky girl I met at school is nowhere to be seen.

'Yeah,' Soren responds, his voice dark and surly.

'How's the surveillance going?'

'Fine. The cameras on sub-level 10 are all looping old footage.'

'Great. Henry Moore isn't here, I need you to try and find him. He should be in a lab somewhere,' she says.

'Okay, checking now.' The comm goes quiet for several moments before we get a response. 'Oh yeah, he's here all right. They've got him up on sub-level 1.'

'Shit,' April swears.

'What's wrong?'

'He's up on a high-level security floor.' She stops talking as she thinks it through. 'Soren, I need you down here.'

April disengages her comm. 'Elle, you take Lara to level 2 above ground. When you get there you will follow the corridor to the end of the hallway and go into the room at the end on the right. Comm Sebastian from there and he'll come and get you both out.'

'Don't you need help?' I ask.

'I'll have Soren and we'll be fine.' She presses her badge against the sensor on the lift and the doors open. 'If anything happens, we're rendezvousing back at the apartment where we changed earlier. Do you remember how to get there?'

'Yeah, I think so.' I slowly help ease Lara off the ground and guide her to the lift. 'C'mon Lara, we're going to get you out of here. April's going to get your dad and we will meet up with them outside.'

She nods shyly and sticks close to me as we enter the lift.

'I'll see you soon,' April says, as the doors close.

The lift ascends swiftly and Lara doesn't say a word the entire ride. Her arms are crossed over her body and she keeps her hair hanging over her face. I don't know what they've done to make her this way. What I do know is they'll pay for it.

The doors open on a bright corridor, which has a deep navy carpet on the floor and a long window at the far end.

We exit the lift and move hastily down the corridor. I glance over my shoulder as the lift door closes behind us. I feel too exposed up here and there are so many doors. We could be caught in an instant. We're nearly to the end, when I hear the sound of a doorknob turning.

'Quickly,' I whisper to Lara, but I know it's too late when I hear the sound of the door shutting behind us.

'Elle? Lara?' We both freeze on the spot and slowly turn to see Hunter who stands there in the centre of the corridor, his face filled with shock.

'What are you doing here?'

CHAPTER TWENTY-NINE

'What am I doing here? What are you doing here?' I ask. Hunter looks just as I remember him, but he seems smarter. His rugged blonde hair has been combed and his shirt has been pressed. Something flickers in my mind, a brief memory that fights to rise to the surface, but it quickly disappears and I shake my head as though to clear it.

Lara shies back behind me and I squeeze her hand reassuringly.

'There's no time for that,' Hunter replies. 'You can't be here. We need to get you both out of here. I know a way, but we have to be quick.'

I glance at the window behind us, and the door we're meant to go through to comm Sebastian from. I don't want to put him in any danger though, and if Hunter knows a way out that has to be a better option.

'Okay,' I respond, but Lara shakes her head. 'C'mon Lara, it's Hunter. Do you remember him?' She shakes her head again.

'He's going to help us get out of here. We can trust him.'

She looks hesitant, but doesn't shake her head again.

'Let's go' I say, facing Hunter.

He gives me a brief nod. 'This way,' he says, walking down the hallway and opening one of the doors. Inside is a stairwell, but instead of going down the stairs he leads us up.

'Are you sure this is the way?' I ask.

'Definite,' he replies.

We walk up two flights of stairs before Hunter pauses by the door to level 4. He slowly opens the door a crack before peering out into the hallway beyond. Once he's certain it's clear, he moves out into the hallway, waving for us to follow. I glance over my shoulder as we leave the stairwell. We haven't seen any recruiters yet, which has to be a good sign.

'So, why are you here?' I whisper to Hunter. 'What happened to you the night we went to the north?'

He shakes his head and raises one finger to his lips as we creep down the hallway, being careful not to make a sound.

When we get to a set of double doors, he twists the knob slowly and carefully pushes the door open. He peeks his head through the door, then waves for us to follow. I let Lara go in first and then once I'm through I close it silently behind us.

'Look who I found,' Hunter says, raising his voice.

I freeze and slowly turn around to face the room. Before me is a huge office, with walls covered in bookshelves and a large wooden desk in the centre. Behind the desk, sits a man who barely glances up at us before waving us away with the flick of a hand.

'I have no use for the girl now. Her father is already doing what we want. Return her to her cell.'

'No,' Hunter says. 'The other one. It's Elle Winters.'

The man's keen eyes slowly rise from the tablet on his desk to my face. His eyes widen with recognition and his upper lip curls into a menacing grin of satisfaction as he fully focuses on me. I gasp. I've seen his navy suit and slicked back blonde hair before. I'd know the evil look in his eyes anywhere. It's the man who watched my MRI scan in the hospital from behind the glass, the man who haunted my nightmares.

My eyes dart away from his and land on the tarnished nameplate on his desk. Joseph Blake, I read, causing my heart to race.

'C'mon, Lara.' I grab her and pull her back towards the door. I throw it open and go to run, but a recruiter stands there and before I can even try to get past him I am thrown back into the room, falling heavily to the floor.

'It's better not to try and run,' Hunter says.

'Why would you turn us in?' I yell at him.

'Because we need you,' he replies.

'We? Since when are you a part of all this?'

'It's always been we,' he says, walking towards me. He crouches down low beside me. 'My father and I needed Lara to convince Henry to help us. And you? Well, you're the added bonus we didn't realise we were looking for.'

'Father?' I ask.

'You were the perfect way to get Lara to the Reintegration Centre where she'd be overpowered. After she managed to slip the recruiters at the Loft, I knew I'd need to try something different.'

'But you helped me ... I trusted you...'

Something flickers across his eyes as I say this, and the Hunter who had been my friend, who had helped me so many times, seems to shine out of them. His eyes grow dark again though. 'You were just a play thing to me.'

'I don't believe that.'

'Enough!' Joseph bellows. 'Hunter? Have one of the recruiters take Lara back to her cell and take Elle to sub-level one. Try not to be as rough with her as you were with Lara. That girl's nearly lost her mind and we need Elle healthy.'

Hunter nods to the recruiter by the door, who grabs Lara by the arm and pulls her from the room. Lara's voice breaks as she screams and I can still hear her petrified sobs as she is dragged down the corridor.

My heart hardens and I feel a cold detachment pulsing through me as I listen to her cries. Images force their way to the surface of my mind and time seems to slow as Hunter turns to face me.

It has felt like a segment of my mind has been barricaded for so long, but the bricks that form the wall crumble as Hunter looks into my eyes. I gasp as my consciousness is pulled from the present and into a dreamlike state. It's almost as if the room around me dissolves and, instead of the white walls of Joseph's office, I am surrounded by memories that were locked away from me these past months.

I'm inside a white cell and I can see another version of myself cowering in the corner of the room. I recognise the place immediately. It's the room I dreamt of in the hospital with the man cloaked in shadow. The place still gives me nightmares, but this time as I watch the dream play out I feel like an outsider, looking in.

When the door opens to reveal the man in shadow, I take an unconscious step backward from where I watch. My heart races because there is a difference with him. This time when I look through the doorway there is no shadow to cover his face. I can clearly see the man who enters the room to torment me. It's not Joseph, but Hunter.

He slowly closes in on my shaking form in the corner of the room. 'You have to understand Elle, we need your cooperation and if you aren't going to help us we'll have to find another way,' he croons, as he approaches me.

'Help you? You abandoned me in North Hope and sent recruiters to find me. You've spent weeks tormenting me in here. I won't help you.'

Hunter frowns and for a moment a look of concern crosses his eyes, but he quickly pushes it away. 'I'm giving you one last chance Elle. Do what you've been asked.'

'What if I don't?' I ask, my voice deep and my words spat through my teeth.

'You will forget these last weeks and when you wake up, we'll try again. There will be no more fighting and we'll make it so you're more than happy to help.'

'I will never help you monsters.'

He shakes his head, smiling. 'Yes, you will, and you'll be happy to.'

'I will make you pay for this,' I growl.

Hunter doesn't respond. He merely holds one hand out towards me. 'This won't hurt one bit...'

I shake my head as recalled pain sears through my mind, which jolts my consciousness back into the present. Barely a moment has passed since I was pulled into the memory, but it only took a moment to finally learn the truth. Hunter was the one to take away my memories of the hospital. He left me in North Hope and raised the alarm.

Hunter reaches towards me and I feel a wave of pure hatred for him. 'I'm sorry our reunion hasn't gone how you probably hoped,' he says.

'Hunter?' I make him pause with his arm reached out to me. 'I hope I never see your face again.' I wrench the inhibitor band off my wrist and clamp my hand down on his outstretched arm, screaming out in pain as the raw energy of my talent rips through my body and pushes out through every pore in my skin. I feel like I'm on fire and the pain is so intense I can't tell if I'm hot or cold. I squint my eyes shut as burning tears pour from them. I hear glass shattering and a roaring noise, followed by a thousand screams of terror.

My body shudders as powerful tremors shake the ground beneath me and waves of nausea roll in my belly. When the ground stops shaking and the pain I feel begins to subside, I slowly open my eyes and find the entire office is covered in ice. Joseph is frozen at his desk and Hunter has become a statue beside me, his face contorted in pure pain. I jump back from him.

'Hunter?' My lower lip trembles as I stare into his frozen eyes, but they don't stare back. They are as lifeless as the rest of his body.

I slowly edge myself backwards, dragging my body away from him, towards the door. What have I done? I rub my face and when I pull my hand away it is covered in blood from my nose. The sight causes me to whimper and I rub my face frantically with the sleeve of my top.

I try to stand, to get as far away from what I've done as I can, but my legs collapse beneath me. Instead of hitting the floor though, I find two arms wrapped around me.

'Elle? Are you okay?' Sebastian asks.

'Don't come near me!' I try to get out of his arms, but my attempts at escape are too weak and his arms hold steady around me. I crumble into them and sob. My heart feels as ice cold as the two men I just doomed, and each sob seems to put a splintering crack through the centre of it. I am a monster.

As I cry I feel a biting cold touch my skin and when I look around I find we're outside, down a side alley that looks onto the square.

'What have I done?' I whisper to Sebastian. I look beyond him to the screaming crowd in the square and see the bright blue flames that leap from the frosted windows of Joseph's office in the building behind them. I did that.

'You did what you had to. You were brave in there and I'm so proud of you.'

'But Hunter,' I choke on his name, 'Joseph ... what I did to them...'

'It was an accident.'

'It wasn't. He was the reason I lost all my memories in the hospital and I wanted him to hurt for what he'd done to Lara.' I gasp. 'Lara. Oh my god, where's Lara? Was she hurt? Please tell me I didn't hurt her!'

'Who's Lara?'

'Sebastian we have to get back in there! We have to get her out.' My eyes dart between his face and Headquarters.

He frowns and gives a slight shake of his head. 'Elle...' he says, drawing my name out like he's about to say, 'no.'

'She's Henry Moore's daughter. I went to school with her up here and she was captured and imprisoned in that place because of me.' I grasp onto his wrists tightly. 'We found her in there and I can't leave her behind.'

He stills and focuses in on my eyes. 'Where is she?'

'She was ... she was out in the hallway,' I recall. 'Please can you get her?'

He glances at the building behind me, before shaking his head. 'I need to get you out of here. We can't risk going back in.'

'Please Sebastian,' I beg. 'I can't leave her there!'

He hesitates. 'We can't risk it, that place will be swarming with recruiters now, but maybe April can do something.'

I nod frantically, tears welling in my eyes.

He lifts his cuff to his lips. 'April?'

'Sebastian, have you got her out?' April's urgent reply comes through the cuff.

'Yes, Elle's with me now,' he says. 'But, her friend is still in there.'

April swears in response and I can just hear her muttering in the background. 'Okay, Soren's on it. Get Elle back to our meeting point!' The comm cuts out.

I take a deep breath and try to calm myself. They're taking care of Lara. She's going to be okay.

'We need to go,' Sebastian says.

I nod and try to ignore the pulling feeling that seems to thread from my gut to Headquarters. I realise Soren is going to get Lara, but it feels like I'm abandoning her, again.

Sebastian takes my hand and squeezes it firmly. It reassures me more than any words can right now. I move to follow him, but freeze before I take a step. 'Sebastian, I left my inhibitor band in there. I should be locked away so I don't hurt anyone else. *I don't want to hurt anyone else.*' My voice sounds hysteric.

'Just remember what April said and concentrate on your sense of smell. Here,' he puts his hand in his pocket and fishes a small package out, which he passes to me.

'What is this?' I ask, opening it to look inside.

'Coffee beans. When I found out how smell could help you focus I got them just in case you were ever without your inhibitor. I thought you could smell these.'

I take a deep whiff of the pungent smelling beans. The smell is strong, but normal compared with the intense energy I just felt. They are calming and I feel slightly more in control. I throw my arms around him, tears welling in my eyes. 'How can I thank you for this?'

'You just did,' he says, smiling. 'Come on, we need to get you out of here before more recruiters show up.'

CHAPTER THIRTY

The apartment is empty when we return. A part of me hoped the others had somehow made it back before us, but they were still in the building when we left so it was always unlikely they'd beat us here. I pace restlessly, waiting for them to get back. Nerves churn violently in my stomach and my ceaseless pacing doesn't seem to be helping.

When the door handle finally turns, I race for it and barrel into Lara's arms as she enters. 'You got out okay,' I exclaim.

She shyly nods as Soren brushes past her and into the apartment. I catch him muttering as he stalks over to the window and I can tell he's not pleased with having to get Lara out. I help ease Lara onto the floor, and she wraps her arms firmly around her legs, burying her head in them.

I take another whiff of the coffee beans. The sight of Lara is enough to set me off again. It makes me angry to see her this way and it's difficult to keep my feelings under control.

'April's not with you?' Sebastian asks.

Soren simply shakes his head in response.

I stand and watch him closely. 'Well, where is she?'

'She'll be here,' he responds, his eyes firmly on the world outside the window. He doesn't seem bothered she hasn't returned yet.

I cross my arms over my chest and walk across to the window. I can't see Headquarters from here, but I can still see masses of people dressed in purple down on the street. They cover the area and move quickly, herding away from Headquarters in a panic. It's not surprising though, given what I did to it. I just want to get out of here and go back to camp.

'What do you think is taking April so long?'

'I'm not sure. She should be here by now,' Sebastian says, checking the time on his cuff.

I take a deep breath in and slowly blow it out. I wish she would get here already. I just hope she's okay.

'Elle?' Sebastian says, worry tingeing the tone of his voice.

'Yeah?' I ask, turning to look at him. He slowly nods at my hands and I follow his gaze to look at them. Sparks of electricity, similar to tiny lightning strikes dance across my fists.

I gasp, but my fear only seems to make them grow larger.

'What do I do?' I hold my fists out in front of me, terrified to be anywhere near them. I can feel tears welling in my eyes and my body stiffens as I refuse to so much as breathe for fear of doing something wrong and hurting everyone.

'Come here,' Sebastian says.

I shake my head. 'I don't want to hurt you.'

'Just come here.'

I notice Soren backing away out of the corner of my eye. Even he seems afraid of me. I need to get out of here. Away from Lara and Sebastian before I hurt either of them.

I can feel the untamed energy pulsing through me again. It almost seems to ripple just under my skin as though looking for a way to break free.

Sebastian takes purposeful steps towards me. 'Elle?'

I take a step backwards and find my back against the window. 'Don't come any closer!'

'I'm going to keep coming closer, will you please just look me in the eyes?'

I look up and into his blue eyes. There's not a touch of fear there as he looks back. Only concern and worry for me. He takes another step closer.

'Stop. I don't want to hurt you,' I plead.

'You won't because I believe in you, and if you had half the belief in yourself that I have, you would be able to control this.'

'I can't...'

'Yes, you can.' He steps closer again. He's only a few feet from me now, so close that one of the sparks could easily stray and hurt him.

'I'm a monster.'

'No, you're Elle, my Elle. The Elle who hates video games and yet always manages to beat me on Speed Racer, the Elle who has always been obsessed with old movies because they give her hope. You're the Elle who spent our childhood playing doctor because she was determined to help save people one day. You are not a monster. Not even close.'

He takes a step closer and slowly lowers his hands and wraps them around mine. I gasp and look down, but the electricity is gone and all that is left is his hands around mine. He leans forward and places a kiss on my forehead.

'You will get control of this one day and, until you do, I'll be here to hold your hand.'

'How did you stop it?'

'Because I know you would never hurt me. Come on, let's go sit down and wait for April. We need to keep you calm until she gets here and can help you.'

We wait for hours for April to appear and it's long after nightfall before Soren suggests the unthinkable.

'What if she didn't make it out?'

'Don't be stupid, she'll be here,' Sebastian says.

'We've tried comming her a dozen times and she hasn't answered. What if they have her and are torturing her for our location right now?'

'She'll be here,' Sebastian says, through gritted teeth.

I nod, agreeing with him. 'She'll be back. I know she will.' I don't know if it's wishful thinking, or a talent I didn't know I had, but I feel it deep in my gut she's fine and will be here any time now.

Another hour passes before I hear the elevator doors open out of the apartment and down the hallway. 'Did you hear that?' I ask Sebastian.

He shakes his head. 'Stay here.' He slowly eases himself off the ground and makes his way towards the front door of the apartment.

There are several sets of footsteps in the hallway, but I can't tell how many people are out there. They stop by the front door and I hear the sound of the doorknob as it slowly turns and the door creaks open.

'Oh, thank god it's you,' Sebastian exclaims.

'Who else would it be?' April responds. She comes into view, looking weary. Following her is a man in his fourties, who I assume is Lara's father, and Jess, Lara's sister. Jess and the man rush over to Lara, who doesn't cower away from them like she has with the rest of us since we rescued her. The three of them huddle together, comforting each other.

'Sorry it took us so long. We had to go to get Jess,' April says.

'She was in there too?' I ask.

'No, but only because the recruiters didn't know she was on the surface.'

'How is that even possible?'

'I didn't realise this was a family expedition,' Soren interrupts, from the corner of the room.

'It wasn't,' April replies. 'But we had to retrieve them both.'

He raises one eyebrow and leans back against the wall. 'Because...'

'It's none of your concern why,' she replies. 'All you need worry about now is helping us get back to camp.'

Soren looks like he wants to argue with April, but doesn't say a word.

'What happened back there?' April asks me.

'You saw that?' I ask.

'Everyone saw it,' she responds.

'So you know what I did...'

'Elle, it's not so bad.'

'I killed two people!' My voice shakes as I admit the truth I've been struggling to accept myself. I haven't dared thinking about it for fear of how my talent would react. Even now I can feel it humming beneath the surface of my skin.

'No, you didn't. Hunter and Joseph are fine. Recruiters got to them quickly and were able to revive them.'

'They're fine?'

She nods. 'Yeah. They're going to be okay.'

I wrap my arms around my stomach and let out a long breath I didn't even know I was holding. I feel relieved I didn't kill them, but anxious at the same time. Knowing they're still alive gives me a bad feeling.

'Are you sure they survived?' I ask.

She glances at Sebastian uncomfortably, before looking back at me. 'Joseph just released a news announcement about our attack. He's alive.'

'What did he say?' Sebastian asks.

'Just that this action wouldn't be tolerated and he would hunt down the culprits.' She looks uneasy about his statement and her words chill me. If he's seeking revenge I'm the first person he will come for.

'We should get moving back to camp,' April continues, trying not to look at me directly.

As we gather together to leave the building I pull April aside. 'Did you know the truth about Hunter and who his father was?' I ask.

She nods. 'I knew who his father was, but I didn't know he was involved like this.'

'Why didn't you ever tell me?'

'Because I didn't realise how close he'd gotten to you.'

I cross an arm over my chest and rub my eyes tiredly with my other hand. 'It doesn't make any sense why he was helping me find Sebastian. Back at Headquarters he said he was only using me to get to Lara.'

She smiles sadly. 'C'mon, we better get these guys back to camp.' She nods her head over my shoulder, in the direction of Lara's family.

I turn and smile as I watch the three of them together. At least one good thing has come from tonight.

Sebastian moves to stand with us. 'I think everyone's about ready to leave,' he says.

April glances at Lara and her family before facing us. 'There's something you should know before we go,' she says. 'Jess is not Lara's sister.'

'What do you mean?'

'She's her mum.'

I look back to Lara and her family. Jess looks so young, how can that even be possible? Unless...

'She doesn't age?' I ask, turning back to April. 'Jess, she doesn't age?'

April nods her head. 'Henry explained when we went to get her. Lysartium changed Jess' cells in such a way that when they replicate they no longer mutate at all.'

'Which means...'

'Yep, that's right,' she says, slinging her arm over my shoulder. 'You are looking at one bona fide key to the cure.'

CHAPTER THIRTY-ONE

Discarded purple ribbons and confetti whisk across the empty street outside the apartment building. The crowds of people dispersed hours ago and the dark and empty road has taken on an abandoned quality.

'I don't have my inhibitor anymore,' I tell April, as we leave the safety of the apartment building and step into the street. I feel calmer than I had earlier, but I suspect April is having a lot to do with that.

'It doesn't matter, we can get you a new one back at camp.'

'What if I hurt someone before then?'

'You won't. I'll make sure of it,' she says, smiling at me confidently.

'There's no way you can be sure.' I lightly touch her wrist, causing her to slow her walk and fall back with me so we are several feet from the rest of the group. When I'm certain no one can hear us, I continue. 'I've been thinking all afternoon about what I did. I don't want to hurt anyone again.'

'You won't—'

'Don't say I wont! I will and we both know it. It doesn't matter what I do or how I try, these talents are too much for me. I don't want them and if Henry knows of a way to get rid of them. I want it.'

'You would give them up?'

I nod. 'I was never meant to be talented; I was engineered by doctors to be this way. Even in the brief moments where I feel like I have control, deep down I know I don't. Sebastian keeps trying to tell me to believe in myself and control will come, but I don't think that's the case. I don't think it's possible.'

April frowns. 'You've seen what you can do when I help you, which only proves it is possible. Try not to focus on the big picture. Maybe just focus on figuring out the smaller things first.'

'But if they figure out a way to fix us, will you make sure I can get it? I don't want these talents now I've seen what I can do. I don't want to be a weapon.'

'Okay,' she says. '*If* they figure it out, you'll be first in line, but please don't put all your hopes into this. The cure is supposed to stop mutations, not get rid of them.'

'Even if it would only stop me from absorbing new talents, I want it.'

She sighs and gives me a nod. We move to catch up with the others. Sebastian gives me a questioning look, but I merely shake my head. I don't want to talk about this with him right now.

'How did you stay hidden from the recruiters?' I ask Jess, in an attempt to draw the attention away from me.

She glances up at Henry, who has one arm wrapped around her and the other around Lara, and gives him a small smile. 'Henry was the lead scientist in the ARC and knew about the surface and talents. When he discovered my mutation and realised I was no longer aging, we decided the best course of action would be to bring me to the surface off the records. We couldn't keep what was happening to me hidden in the ARC.'

'And no one suspected?'

She shakes her head.

'And you'll never get old?' Sebastian asks.

'From what we can tell,' Henry replies.

April purses her lips as she watches Jess. 'I haven't heard of anyone with anything like it.'

Jess shrugs. 'We know so little about these talents, who knows what we'll see in the future.'

The thought of what talents are yet to come causes a shiver to run down my spine. I hate to think how they'll end up if Joseph continues his experiments in the hospital.

WHEN WE REACH the fence that borders the air base and start to move across the open plain towards the second hangar, I can hear a soft whimpering noise almost whispered on the wind.

'Did you hear that?' I ask Sebastian, who shakes his head. The sound was haunting and disturbing enough to make the hairs on my arms stand on end.

'Something's wrong,' I whisper to him.

'What?' he asks.

'I don't know yet.'

As we get closer to camp the noise becomes louder and I notice movement up ahead, near to the second hangar we walk through to get to camp. I squint my eyes, concentrating determinedly on my sight, which zooms in on the building.

'Kelsey!' I gasp, as I catch sight of her standing by the door. I start to run, but Sebastian catches me by the elbow and we blink out of existence, appearing next to her in a second.

I crouch down beside her and take her small hands in mine. 'Kels what's wrong? Why are you out here? Why aren't you back at camp?'

Her lower lip quivers and tears run down her face.

'Kelsey?'

'There was a bad man,' she whispers, so softly you'd need talented hearing to catch it.

'What bad man?'

She shakes her head, refusing to meet my eyes.

'It's okay, you can tell me.'

'Shit ... Elle!' Sebastian shouts.

I pick Kelsey up in my arms and run over to Sebastian who stands at the large open mouth of the hangar. I'm almost to him, when I catch the undeniable scent of smoke in the air. I sprint the last few steps.

'No!' I scream, as the trees come into view. The forest near the clinic is ablaze, with flames leaping from tree to tree. It appears small now, but looks to be catching quickly. The others catch up to us and gasp as they set their eyes on the fire before us.

'What do we do?'

'C'mon,' Sebastian says. 'We need to get closer, make sure everyone's okay.'

I leave Kelsey with Lara and her family and we start running in the direction of the fire, which only flares up higher, the closer we get. When we reach the trees we move through them carefully to the camp, avoiding patches that have already caught alight. Soren and April head for the control tent, while Sebastian and I race for the clinic. We are almost there when I catch sight of a column of flames up ahead.

'The clinic is on fire!' I yell to Sebastian, as I instinctively run faster, desperate to get to the place that holds my friends.

What if they were caught inside? My stomach turns and my talent pulses under my skin as I think the unthinkable. Without April with us to control me I take deep breaths in through my nose and concentrate on the smell of smoke to calm me. I can't afford to mess up here.

As we reach the clinic a wave of relief rushes over me when I see a group of people standing out front of it, keeping back from the blaze. We rush over to them.

'Did everyone get out okay?' I ask the first doctor we meet.

He nods. 'Yes, we all got out of the clinic fine. It was the last place to catch fire. Some of the others in camp weren't so lucky.'

I nod grimly, not daring to think of the people who didn't make it out. Not now. We move past the man and start searching for our friends.

So many people have ashen faces and cough as they try to clear their lungs from the smoke. I catch sight of Aiden and Jane at the edge of the group. Aiden has her lying on a soft patch of grass and is holding her hand.

'You're both okay!' I exclaim, rushing over to him.

He smiles sadly. 'Yes, we're okay.'

'Where's Will?' I ask, looking around and expecting to find him nearby.

His face falls and a small frown comes on his forehead. 'I'm ... I'm not too sure. I thought one of the other doctors got him out.'

I turn away from Aiden. 'Will?' I yell out.

'What's wrong?' Sebastian asks, rushing over.

Panic surges through me. 'Will's not here.'

'I'm sure he's fine,' Sebastian says. He seems confused but, catching the look in my eyes, he nods with understanding. He may be fine, but until I find him, I won't be.

'Will?' I yell, louder than before. I rush from person to person asking them if they've seen him, but no one has, not since before the fire.

I stop in front of the clinic. What if he's still inside? What if somebody missed him?

'Elle, you can't go in there!' Sebastian pleads.

'What if he's in there? What if he's stuck inside?'

'I'm sure he's out here.'

'No, you're not! No one's seen him since before this started.'

'You can't go in there, it's too dangerous,' he insists.

I almost agree with him. I almost listen to him, but then I hear a faint cry. One lone and desperate sob from inside the building. It's so quiet that if you were breathing too loudly you could miss it, but I feel certain of what I've heard.

'Elle!' Sebastian screams as I run towards the burning building. 'Don't!'

His voice tugs at me, begs me not to run inside, but I can't stop myself. I run to the clinic, ignoring the flames that flare overhead. They spit and hiss as they consume the walls and engulf the roof of the building. Will's inside, I know it.

I push through the front door and my eyes immediately begin to water as I enter and the thick black smoke engulfs me. I pull my top up to cover my mouth and nose, but it barely does anything to help me breathe.

A hand grabs mine causing me to jump.

'Sebastian? What are you doing in here?' I say, coughing as I inhale a breath of smoke.

'C'mon, we'll find him quicker together.'

I nod and together we move forward. Flames cover the walls inside and the heat is as suffocating as the smoke that engulfs us. My lungs burn and my forehead sweats as we continue further inside. Several loose poles have fallen from the ceiling and lay at odd angles across the floor. Sebastian teleports us past one that is blocking the way and I rush over to Will's bed, but it's empty.

'Where else would he be?' Sebastian asks.

'I don't know, I ... the back office. There's a rat back there he's obsessed with. He must've gone back for it.'

'Right.' Sebastian grabs my hand and I feel the welcome, biting cold for an all too brief second as he teleports us to the back room.

'Will?' I yell into the room. It's so thick with smoke, I can barely breathe and I can't see anything in here.

I take a step forward and knock something with my foot. I bend down and see a small cage. I fall to my hands and knees feeling around for Will. He's got to be here, he's ... a hand. I feel a hand. It's Will, it has to be.

'I've got him!' I cry out to Sebastian, causing me to cough again. I try to shake Will awake, but he's out completely. Sebastian crouches next to me and takes Will's hand.

'I'll be right back for you,' he says, before disappearing with Will.

I grasp onto the cage and try to stand, but I feel weak and sleepy.

I close my eyes and try to concentrate on Sebastian. He will be back for me at any second. I just need to hold out until then.

They'll be on the grass outside by now. They'll be able to see the starry night overhead and the blazing inferno that I'm in. The image seems so real; I feel like I could almost reach my hand out and touch it.

I feel a tugging sensation in my belly button and my skin feels tingly all over. I'm hit by a sudden, brief sensation of freezing cold and when I open my eyes I'm outside, standing beside Sebastian with the rat cage in my hands.

'You came back for me,' I say, smiling deliriously before staggering forward unsteadily on my feet.

Sebastian wraps his hand around my arm to support me and rubs my back softly. 'Actually, you decided not to wait.'

'I don't understand,' I say, turning to look at him. His face is out of focus and my vision is blurry. 'Is Will okay?' I ask, shaking my head in an attempt to clear my vision.

'He'll be just fine thanks to you.' Sebastian's voice sounds distant as he answers, as my attention is caught by something on the side of the clinic building.

'Do you see that?' I say, staggering as I try to maintain my feet. I collapse down onto the ground as darkness encircles me, dragging my consciousness towards sleep. But before I pass out I see it clearly; words on the side of the building that have been shaped by the very flames that destroy it.

'You froze my house, I'll burn yours.'

CHAPTER THIRTY-TWO

'Elle? Can you hear me?'

I groan and try to open my eyes, but I still feel trapped in sleep. My body is so tired it almost tingles with exhaustion.

'Elle?'

'She'll probably be groggy for a while,' another voice says.

My senses slowly awaken. My throat burns and I'm overcome by the hubbub of voices surrounding me. It's hard to ignore the cacophony of sounds that fight for attention in my mind.

'Where am I?' I croak, slowly blinking my eyes open and attempting to sit up.

'You're in one of the hangars,' Sebastian says, squeezing my hand. My ears draw in on the sound of his voice, lessening the overly loud ambient noises that try to overwhelm me.

'How do you feel?' he asks, holding a glass of water out to me. Seeing the liquid inside makes me realise how desperately thirsty I am.

'Water...' I rasp. Sebastian lifts the glass to my lips and I greedily drink the cool water inside. It only helps calm the pain in my throat for a moment, but it's better than nothing. When I've drained the glass I look up at him. 'I feel like someone's hit me with a car and pushed a hot poker down my throat, but I'll live.'

I look around the room at all the people camped out inside. Most are talking quietly amongst themselves and some are sleeping on the ground using spare clothes as pillows. There's a strong undercurrent of loss in the room and I can almost feel it rubbing against my skin.

'What happened?'

'Don't you remember? There was a fire.' Aiden's voice is soothing, but I can see there's worry in his eyes at my forgetfulness.

'The fire, of course.' I rub my eyes as images of the fire flash through my thoughts. 'Do we know how it started? Is everyone okay?'

Sebastian glances uneasily at Aiden. 'It was Joseph, that's all we know for the moment. He took M before it all started.'

'He took M?' They both nod. 'But how did he find us? I thought we were safe here.' I look between the two of them, but they seem uncertain.

Sebastian blows out a long sigh and rubs his forehead. 'April thinks they got the information from someone who was working on the inside. Either a mole here, or they could have found and interrogated one of our people who have been placed undercover in the government. She's called everyone back in and if anyone's missing...'

'They'll go straight to the top of the suspect list,' I finish for him.

'Exactly,' Sebastian replies.

'Do you have any idea where they took M?'

'No, but we'll find out and get him back.'

I take another sip of water to cool my throat and look around the room for my friends. Lara is sitting in the corner with Kelsey, while her parents walk around helping people who were injured in the fire. April's talking heatedly with Soren by the entrance of the hangar, but there's one face I can't spot anywhere.

'Where's Will?' I ask.

Sebastian hesitates and looks to Aiden for a response.

'He still hasn't woken up,' Aiden says.

'He's going to be okay, right?'

'I don't know,' he replies. 'He inhaled a lot of smoke before you got him out and we haven't got the equipment we need to help him. It all went in the fire. It's going to be a matter of waiting.'

'Surely there's something...' My voice trails off as Aiden shakes his head sadly. 'Can I see him?'

'You need more rest.'

'I'll be fine. Where is he?' I persist.

'I'll take you there now.'

Sebastian helps stand me up and I use him for support as I follow Aiden. We walk to the back of the room, where Will is lying on a stretcher that has been placed on the ground. He is so still as he lies there, his chest barely rising to breathe. His face and clothes are smudged with ash, and he looks vulnerable and alone.

I sit down next to him and take his hand in mine. I've seen him sleeping so many times before and he looks no different now. He seems like he could wake up at any moment.

'I'm monitoring him closely and I'll need to do another examination of you in a while. I'll be back to check on you both in a bit,' Aiden says, turning to leave. Sebastian squeezes my shoulder and follows him, leaving us alone.

I want to say something comforting to Will, I want to tell him everything is going to be alright, but the words fail to come to me. So, instead, I sit there simply being with him, holding his hand tightly in mine, waiting for him to wake up.

SOMEONE SHAKES my shoulder and I jerk upwards from where my head was resting on Will's lap. I hadn't realised I'd fallen asleep. Will's hand is still firmly in mine, but it feels colder now, harder.

'Will?' I ask, but he is still firmly asleep.

'Elle?' I look over my shoulder in response to find Aiden there.

'Sorry, I know I shouldn't have fallen asleep,' I say, 'but I was so tired. Have you given Will his check up yet? How is he?'

Aiden kneels down next to me and takes a hold of my shoulder. 'Elle, he's gone.'

'What do you mean he's gone?' The words don't make sense. He's right here. I'm holding his hand. He hasn't gone anywhere. My blood runs cold as the words start to make sense. 'No...'

I turn back to face Will and take a hold of his arm, shaking it gently. 'Will? You have to wake up now.' His body holds stiff though. 'C'mon, you have to wake up!' I urge him more forcefully.

'Elle, he's not going to wake up,' Aiden says. He's trying to talk sense into me, I know he is, but I don't want to hear it.

'No!' I yell at him. 'C'mon Will, please wake up, *please*.' My body starts to shake and tears slowly trickle down my cheeks. A breeze seems to pick up inside the room, buffeting my clothes against my body and whipping my hair around my face. It whisks around the two of us, like a slowly building storm that gathers momentum with us in the eye of it.

'Can someone get April in here?' I hear Aiden yell, but the sound is muted and my ears are filled with a blocked ringing noise as adrenaline and pain surges through my body. Strong gusts push and pull at me, whipping violently across my skin, but I barely notice them. My attention is focused solely on the small boy lying so still before me.

I don't understand how he can be gone. He looks completely fine. There doesn't look like there's anything wrong with him, he just looks like he's sleeping. I look down at his cold hand in mine. It's no longer simply cold, but frozen in my grasp.

I gasp and yank my hand from his. 'No ... no, no, no. What have I done?'

'Elle, it's okay,' someone says.

I shake my head and wipe the tears under my eyes. 'I'm so sorry Will.'

'It's not working, I can't control her,' April says, from behind me.

I whip my head around to look at her, but the total fear I see in her eyes shocks me, and awakens me from the sea of emotions I am drowning in. The wind stops and the world becomes silent in its wake.

'Are you okay?' she asks me, her voice unusually timid.

I nod and wipe my cheeks with the back of my hands. My shoulders slouch and I wrap my arms around my body as I glance back at Will. 'He's gone.'

April nods and her eyes drop to the floor. 'He's gone.'

CHAPTER THIRTY-THREE

We hold a small funeral for Will the following afternoon. No one in the camp knew him, besides our small group. They never got the chance to. The sun shines brightly overhead as we lower his body into the ground.

'He would love the spot you picked,' April says to me, as we stand and watch the boys who are just about finished shovelling dirt onto his grave. The trees in this area of forest have lush, green leaves and bright blue wild flowers bloom all over the grass that grows in the small meadow.

'I found it when I went for a walk a few days ago,' I say, smiling sadly. 'Once he was better, I planned to bring him here as a surprise.'

April puts her arm around me and rests her head on my shoulder. 'You can't blame yourself for what happened,' she says.

'I don't,' I whisper in reply. 'There is only one person who did this and I wish I'd killed him when I had the chance.'

'Don't say that!'

'Why not? I was beginning to think I was a monster, but compared to Joseph I'm not bad at all. He needs to be dealt with.'

April pulls back from me and eyes me seriously. 'He will be, in time. Right now, we need to focus on the cure and getting M back.'

I nod and try to calm my breathing, but the cure is the last thing on my mind right now. I feel so angry over what has happened, all I want is revenge.

'Are you any closer to working out how Joseph found us?' I ask.

April sighs and rubs her forehead tiredly. 'No. A few people still haven't reported back. Someone may have been taken in and questioned, or worse, one of our own could have given us up. We don't know yet.

'So where do we go from here?' I ask.

'We will have to relocate. We have a backup location, but with M gone and the culprit who gave us away not found, I don't think it's safe to go there yet. We'll have to find somewhere else.'

'How long will that take? Will we be safe here?'

She shakes her head. 'I don't know. I think the South Hope ruins are our best bet until we find somewhere safer.' She seems worried, but I don't know what to say.

I take her hand in mine. 'That sounds like a good plan for now. We just need to focus on getting everyone away from here as quickly as we can.'

She nods her head along with me, as though wanting to believe it's true. 'You're right,' she agrees.

She looks over at Aiden and Sebastian who both stand, leaning on their shovels, looking at Will's grave. 'We should probably head back,' she says, addressing the three of us.

'You guys go. I wouldn't mind a minute alone,' I reply.

The boys move to leave, but April hangs back. 'I almost forgot,' she pulls an inhibitor band from her pocket and passes it to me.

I take the device and hold it lightly between my fingers. 'Thanks,' I reply, looking between the inhibitor and April.

She gives me a small smile and turns to follow the others back into the forest. Once they've gone I walk over the Will's grave and sit next to it. I brush my hands over the dirt and place a flower that I picked on top of it.

I haven't been near a grave before. I've never been there when anyone has died. I try to think of what words I should say aloud to Will, and how I could possibly say goodbye, but I don't believe he'd hear me now. It wouldn't change what happened and it certainly won't bring him back.

I continue to toy with the inhibitor in my fingers. A part of me wants to put it back on and to feel it safely around my wrist again, but something stops me. The band keeps me in control, but it weakens me. It keeps the beast inside me tame, but maybe it shouldn't be caged.

I feel a mixture of feelings at war inside of me, but as soon as I think of Joseph and what he's done to Will, my insides turn cold.

'Goodbye Will,' I whisper, placing one hand on the soil of his grave in farewell.

I slowly stand and move away, refusing to look back at the beautiful meadow, for fear of changing my mind. I already know what I'd see there—the sun dancing across the smooth glass surface of the inhibitor band I've left behind.

~

END OF BOOK THREE

~

Continue in book 4: Destined
Available here!

ACKNOWLEDGMENTS

I would like to express my gratitude to you, the reader. You are the reason I write and I am so pleased you decided to continue with Elle's story in *Fractured*. I hope you have enjoyed reading these books as much as I enjoyed writing them.

Thank you to everyone who has posted reviews and used social media to help promote the series. I appreciate each and every review and post, and any success I have is in large part a result of your endorsement.

This book would not have been possible without the encouragement of my family. I am so lucky to have the support of such amazing individuals.

Finally, to Pete, your contribution has been immeasurable. You inspire me to be a better writer each and every day—not to mention, when my writing sucks you fix it!

ALSO BY ALEXANDRA MOODY

ABOUT THE AUTHOR

ALEXANDRA MOODY is an Australian author. She studied Law and Commerce in her hometown, Adelaide, before going on to spend several years living abroad in Canada and the UK. She is a serious dog-lover, double-black-diamond snowboarder and has a love/hate relationship with the gym.

Never miss a release!
Sign up at: www.subscribepage.com/TheARCsubscribe

For more information:
www.alexandramoody.com
info@alexandramoody.com

Made in the USA
San Bernardino, CA
23 February 2019